"You, my dear sweet wife, are in love with me."

The audacity of the comment was too much to overlook. "I'm what?" Julia asked.

"In love with me," Alek repeated with supreme confidence. "I was a fool not to recognize it earlier."

"You're badly in need of reality therapy," Julia said, making her words as amusing as she could. "That's the most ridiculous thing you've ever said."

"Wait, I promise you it'll get better. Much better."

"Much worse, you mean," she said with an exaggerated yawn. "Now, if you don't mind, I'd like to get some sleep."

"You agreed to be my wife. How long is it going to take before you live up to your end of our bargain? How long, my love?"

Dear Reader,

Last year, I requested that you send me your opinions on the books that we publish—and on romances in general. Thank you so much for the many thoughtful comments. For the next couple of months, I'd like to share with you quotes from those letters. This seems very appropriate now, while we are in the midst of the THAT SPECIAL WOMAN! promotion. Each one of our readers is a special woman, as heroic as the heroines in our books.

This August has some wonderful books coming your way. *More Than He Bargained For* by Carole Halston, a warm, poignant story, is the THAT SPECIAL WOMAN! selection. Debbie Macomber also brings us the first book in her FROM THIS DAY FORWARD series—*Groom Wanted*. MORGAN'S MERCENARIES, Lindsay McKenna's action-packed trio concludes this month with *Commando*. And don't miss books from other favorite authors: Marie Ferrarella, Susan Mallery and Christine Rimmer.

I hope you enjoy this book, and all of the stories to come! Have a wonderful August!

Sincerely,

Tara Gavin
Senior Editor
Silhouette Books

Quote of the Month: ''Romance books provide the escape that is needed from the sometimes crazy and hard-to-live-in world. It takes me away for that three or four hours a day to a place no one else can come into. That is why I read romances. Because sometimes there is not a happy ending, and going to a place where there is can uplift the spirit that really needs it.''

—J. Majeski
New Jersey

DEBBIE MACOMBER

GROOM WANTED

Published by Silhouette Books New York

America's Publisher of Contemporary Romance

To Viola Adler,
my incredible great-aunt

SILHOUETTE BOOKS
300 East 42nd St., New York, N.Y. 10017

GROOM WANTED

Copyright © 1993 by Debbie Macomber

ISBN: 0-373-09831-6

First Silhouette Books printing August 1993

All the characters in this book have no existence outside the
imagination of the author and have no relation whatsoever to
anyone bearing the same name or names. They are not even
distantly inspired by any individual known or unknown to the
author, and all incidents are pure invention.

®: Trademark used under license and registered in the United States
Patent and Trademark Office and in other countries.

Printed in the U.S.A.

Books by Debbie Macomber

DEBBIE MACOMBER

hails from the state of Washington. As a busy wife and mother of four, she strives to keep her family healthy and happy. As the prolific author of dozens of best-selling romance novels, she strives to keep her readers happy with each new book she writes.

A Note from the Author

Dear Reader,

For those of you who've read my Special Edition novels over the years, you may have noticed I have something of a trademark in my books. I love to get my characters married as quickly as possible and then watch them fall in love, struggling each step of the way.

This is what happens with Julia and Aleksandr in *Groom Wanted*. Poor Julia carries a heavy load of guilt and is presented with the opportunity to make up for the past by marrying a young Russian immigrant. Julia never expected to fall in love, and my, oh my, how she struggles against Alek's devotion.

Alek is one of my favorite heroes. He's compassionate, proud and stubborn. Although I made him Russian, he bears a strong resemblance to my own husband of twenty-five years. My grandparents came to the United States from a German-speaking settlement in Russia near the Baltic Sea. I was raised on borscht, sugar kuga and lots of love. In creating Alek, I'm sharing a small part of my own heritage.

FROM THIS DAY FORWARD is going to be a fun trilogy. Each story features a different aspect of marriage first and falling in love second. *Groom Wanted* is a green-card story. My next book, *Bride Wanted* (September), is a mail-order-bride story, and the third novel, *Marriage Wanted* (October), is about a marriage of convenience. I hope you'll enjoy all three. I love to hear from readers, and I'd love to know if you enjoyed this trilogy. You can write to me care of Silhouette Books.

Warmest regards,

Debbie Macomber

Chapter One

Julia Conrad wasn't a patient woman in the best of times, and times were bleak. She paced her office, circling her high-gloss black-lacquer-and-brass desk, her steps sluggish, her thoughts uneasy. She felt so damn helpless. She should have gone with Jerry to the Immigration and Naturalization Service herself rather than wait out their decision.

Rubbing her palms together, she retracted the thought. She was a wreck and the INS people would have instantly picked up on that and it could hurt their case. She couldn't help being anxious. The very life of the company rested in the outcome of this day's hearing. Ultimately she was the one responsible for everything.

In an effort to calm herself she stared out the window of the building her grandfather had built thirty years earlier. The weather seemed to echo her mood. A ceiling of black clouds capped the sky. Thunder roared like an angry grizzly and a flash of lightning briefly brightened the room. The lights flickered.

Julia's reflection was mirrored in the window and she frowned, momentarily mesmerized by the unexpected sight of herself. Her dark hair was swept back from her face and secured with a gold clasp. She wore a crisp dark suit, which conveyed tasteful refinement. She looked cool, calm and calculating, which was an accurate description. Outwardly. Inside she was a mass of nerves and high-strung tension. At twenty-seven she had a pleasant face when she smiled, but she hadn't been doing much of that lately. Not in the past three years, to be exact. Her cheekbones were high, her jaw was strong, but it was her eyes that told the story. Her eyes that revealed her vulnerability and her pain.

The image of herself distressed Julia and she hurriedly glanced away. Sighing, she circled her desk once more while silently praying for patience. She was determined to bring the company back on its feet, to overcome the odds stacked against them. Jerry, her brother, had worked with her, sacrificing his own personal life the way she had hers. They'd met with a handful of small successes. And now this.

Both Julia and Jerry were determined to keep Conrad Industries on its feet. Julia owed her father that much. Jerry revealed such faith in her by volunteering his services. If their situations were reversed, she wasn't sure she would have been so forgiving. But her brother had stuck by her side through all the turmoil and all the pain.

Slowly she lowered her gaze, disturbed by the revelation. She didn't have the time or the inclination to worry about it. If she ever needed a cool head and a cooler heart, it was now. Two years of innovative research were about to be lost because they'd allowed the fate of the company to hinge on the experimentation and ideas of one man. Aleksandr Berinski was a brilliant biochemist. Jerry had met him several years earlier while traveling in Europe and convinced Julia he was the answer to their problems. In retrospect Julia decided her brother was right. Alek's ideas would soon revolutionize the paint industry. Bringing him into the United States had been a bold move on their part, but she hadn't been sorry. Not once.

It had been a gamble hiring Aleksandr Berinski from Prushkin, a small state that had once been part of the vast Soviet empire, and moving him to Seattle—the biggest risk Conrad Industries had ever taken. Now the fate of the company rested in the hands of a hard-nosed immigration official.

Once more Julia chastised herself for not attending the hearing at the district office of the INS. She'd done everything within her power to see to it that Aleksandr's visa would be extended. She'd written a letter explaining his importance to the company, and included documentation to prove Aleksandr Berinski was a man of distinguished merit and ability.

Jerry, who was a damn good corporate attorney, had spent weeks building their case. Professional certifications, affidavits, a copy of Aleksandr's diploma and letters of character reference filled Jerry's briefcase.

To his credit, her brother had warned her there could be problems. It's often difficult to renew an H-2 visa, the type Aleksandr had been granted when he'd entered the United States. The very meaning of the H-2 is one of temporary employment. He'd forewarned her that if it looked as though employment might become permanent, then the INS and the Labor Department would be reluctant to extend the visa.

On top of all that, the case had been assigned to a particularly prickly bureaucrat. Jerry had warned her that the INS agent hearing their case might decide Alek had applied for the temporary visa knowing the job was really permanent, and refuse to grant an extension on principle.

She glanced at her watch again and exhaled with tense impatience. Only a few minutes had passed. Annoyed with herself for the uncharacteristic display of anxiety, she sat down on the white leather chair. Everything was neatly arranged on the top of the polished black desk. The small marble pen stand sat at attention next to the phone. The lambskin-covered address and appointment books were perfectly aligned with everything else. Julia liked her desk and her world under control.

Her phone rang and the unexpectedness of the sound caught her off guard. She reached for the receiver knowing it had to be Jerry.

"Sis," Jerry's cool voice greeted. "I'm phoning from the car. I thought you'd want to know the decision as soon as possible."

"Yes, please."

"I'm afraid it didn't go as well as we'd hoped. The INS has decided not to renew Alek's visa."

Julia felt as if she'd been kicked in the stomach. She closed her eyes and waited until the shock had passed. It wasn't as if she didn't expect it. Her brother had given her fair warning. It didn't help matters any that Aleksandr had no proof of a permanent residence in Prushkin. In the eyes of INS that was a red light indicating he never intended on returning. Furthermore, they were dealing with a bureaucracy. In a fit of worry, Julia had tried to contact the agency herself, reason with them. She'd spent nearly an hour on the phone and didn't speak to a single person. She was forced to listen to one recording after another. Push buttons, listen, push another button. She quickly became lost in a hopeless tangle of buttons and messages.

"When will he have to leave?"

"By the end of the week, when his current visa expires."

"That soon?"

"I'm afraid so."

"Jerry, what are we going to do?" she pleaded.

"I'll talk to you about it as soon as we get back to the office," her brother said in reassuring tones. "Don't worry, I've got a contingency plan."

Nice of him to mention it now, Julia mused. He might have said something to her this morning and saved her all this grief.

Within ten minutes her intercom buzzed and her secretary announced that Jerry was in her outer office. She instructed Virginia to send him in and waited, standing at the window.

Jerry walked in and Aleksandr Berinski followed. Although Aleksandr had been working for Conrad Industries for nearly two years, she'd only talked to him a handful of times and briefly even then. She'd read his weekly reports and been excited by the progress he was making. If he was allowed to continue, Julia didn't doubt that Aleksandr's innovations would put Conrad Industries back on firm financial footing.

It struck home with a crushing weight that she and Jerry had taken on the impossible task of resurrecting the family business, literally from the ashes. She'd decided earlier the line of paints Aleksandr was developing would be called Phoenix. To be so close and lose it all now was more than she could bear. For three long, frustrating years, she'd hung on to the business by wheeling and dealing, trades and promises.

Being aggressive and hardworking had come naturally to her. Jerry possessed the same determination and had been a constant help. If she was cold and sometimes ruthless, she credited it to Roger Stanhope. She'd needed to be, but Julia didn't have any more tricks up her sleeve once Aleksandr returned to Prushkin.

She feared that losing the business would prove a fatal blow to her grandmother, for no one knew better than Julia how fragile Ruth's health had become these past few months.

"You said you have a contingency plan." She spoke crisply, the sound of her steps muffled by the thick wheat-colored carpet as she stalked back to her desk. She leaned forward and averted her gaze from Aleksandr's.

The man disturbed her in ways she didn't understand. He was tall and lanky with impeccable manners. His face wasn't pretty the way Roger's had been, but rawboned and lean. His eyes were dark, the brows arched slightly, and in him she read strength and character. Unwillingly she found her own dark eyes drawn to him and the shadow of a smile crept across his face as their gazes held. She focused her attention on Jerry.

"There is one way," her brother said, with obvious reluctance.

"Now isn't the time to play games, tell me what you're thinking," she burst out anxiously, hardly believing he could be holding something back. Jerry knew as well as she did the company's predicament.

Her brother set down his briefcase and motioned toward the leather chair. "Perhaps you'd best sit down."

"Me?" She noted his voice was strained and that surprised her almost as much as his request.

"You, too, Aleksandr," Jerry advised as he stalked to the farthest reaches of the office.

At his silence, Julia turned toward him and tried to read his features in the gloom of the late afternoon. The storm had darkened the sky, stationing shadows around the room until it resembled a dungeon more than an office in a high rise.

"You're sorely testing my patience. Whatever it is you have to say, do it. You've never felt the need to delicately phrase anything before."

Jerry's gaze traveled from Julia to Aleksandr, and she noticed that his cheeks were flushed. He expelled his breath with a heavily weighted sigh and said, "There's only one legal way I know to keep Aleksandr in the country." Slowly he leveled his uncertain, unwavering gaze on Julia. "You could marry him."

"I was hoping you'd stop by and see me." Julia's grandmother, Ruth Conrad, spoke softly, stretching out her hand toward her. She was sitting up in the bed, her white, thin hair combed into a soft chignon. Ruth was pale, her skin a silky shade of alabaster, her eyes sunken now with age, revealing only an allusion of the depth and beauty that had been hers in years past. She was frail and growing more so daily.

The cool facade Julia wore when dealing with Conrad Industries quickly melted whenever she was with her precious grandmother. She sank gratefully into the chair next to the brass four-poster bed and slipped off her shoes, tucking her nylon-covered feet beneath her.

Visiting Ruth was an escape for her. She left her worries and troubles outside the door and soaked in the solace. Her world was often filled with chaos, but with Ruth she found calm. Whenever she was with her grandmother, Julia exhaled panic and inhaled peace.

The storm, which had been flaunting itself across the heavens most of the afternoon, seemed far removed from this bedroom haven.

"The thunder woke me," Ruth said in a low voice, smiling weakly. "I laid back and I could hear huge kettledrums in the sky. Oh, how they rumbled. Then I had Charles open the drapes so I could look outside. The clouds billowed past like giant puffs of smoke. It made for a marvelous show."

Julia took her grandmother's hand and released a slow, uneven breath. She glanced around the room of this woman who was so near to her heart, and took in the treasures Ruth had chosen to keep at her side. A row of silver-framed pictures rested on the nightstand, next to several prescription bottles. A chintz-covered Victorian chair sat in front of the fireplace, a wool fisherman's afghan draped over the back for when Ruth felt well enough to venture from the bed. The round table beside the chair was covered with a dark velvet cloth with thin black fringe. Julia's picture, one taken shortly after she'd graduated from college, was propped next to the lamp. Julia looked away, unable to look at the naïveté and innocence she saw in herself.

"I'm so pleased you stopped by," Ruth said again.

Julia came most every day, knowing the time left with her grandmother was shrinking. Neither spoke of her death, although it was imminent. Julia was determined to do whatever she could to make these last days with her grandmother as comfortable and happy as possible. It was what kept Julia going day after day. She talked to her grandmother, telling her about Alek's ideas, the innovations he was currently working on. Together they discussed the future and how the entire painting industry was about to change because of Alek's vision. Her grandmother had been as impressed with Alek as Julia was herself. Curiosity had gotten the better of Ruth, and she'd asked to meet Alek. Julia arranged to have Jerry bring Alek over so that their grandmother could talk with him. From what she heard later, the two had gotten along famously.

"I've been meaning to talk to you," Ruth whispered.

How weak she sounded, drained of her strength. "Rest," Julia whispered. "We'll talk later."

Ruth responded with a fragile smile. "I don't have much longer, Julia. A few weeks at the most...."

"Nonsense." The truth was much too painful to face, yet much too persistent to ignore. "You're just overly tired is all. It'll pass."

Ruth's eyes drifted shut, but determination lifted them a moment later. "We need to talk about Roger," her grandmother said softly, insistently.

A muscle in Julia's neck tensed. A cold shiver shimmied down her backbone. "Not...now. Some other time...later, much later."

"Might not...have later. It's best to do it now."

"Grandma, please..."

"He betrayed you, child, and you've held on to that grief all these years. Your pain is killing you just as surely as this bum heart of mine is sucking away my life."

"I don't even think of him anymore," Julia tried to assure her, although it was a small lie. She tried desperately to push every thought of Roger from her mind and her heart, but that wouldn't happen until she'd rebuilt what he'd destroyed.

"Regret is poisoning you like snake venom.... I've watched it happen and been too weak...to help you the way I wanted."

"Grandma, please, Roger is out of my life. I haven't seen him in over a year. What possible good would come of speaking of him now?"

"He's gone...in some ways, but not completely. He failed you."

Julia clenched her teeth. That was one way of putting it, albeit mildly. Roger had failed her. He'd also betrayed, tricked and abandoned her. Dear Lord, when she thought of the way she'd loved him, of the way she'd trusted him, it made her physically ill. Never again would she allow a man to reach her heart. Never again would she give a man the power to manipulate her.

"The time's come to forgive him."

Julia closed her eyes and shook her head. Her grandmother was asking the impossible. A woman didn't forgive the things Roger had done. Nor did she forget. Roger had taught her the most valuable lesson of her life and she wasn't going to turn her back on the humiliation he had caused her. Forgive him? It wasn't humanly possible. She would rather bury herself in her work, insulate her life from love, than pardon Roger.

In many ways she had.

"I want you to love again," Ruth said, but her voice was so weak, so impossibly frail, that Julia had to strain to hear. "I don't know that I'll be able to die in peace, knowing you're so miserable."

"Grandma, how can you say such a thing? Jerry and I are working hard to rebuild the company. We're on the brink of doing truly amazing things. I've told you about them and about everything Aleksandr's done. How can you say I'm miserable...these are the most challenging days of my life."

"None of that means much...not when your yesterdays are imprisoned in your pain. I've waited all these years for you to break free and find love again, it hasn't happened. I...look at you—" she hesitated and tears moistened her ageless eyes "—and my heart aches. I want you to marry, to discover the happiness I found. It's the only thing that's kept me alive. I've waited for your season of suffering to pass...."

"I'll never be able to trust another man."

"You must for your own sake."

"I can't, not after what Roger did, surely you understand, surely you—"

With what must have required supreme effort, Ruth shook her head and raised her hand, cutting Julia off. "I've longed for the day you would proudly introduce me to the man you love. I was hoping it would be Aleksandr...he's such a dear man, and so brilliant. But...I can't wait any longer. My time is short, so...very short." Her eyes drifted closed once more and her head slumped forward.

Julia sat quietly while the seeds of fear took root within her. Love again? Impossible. Out of the question. Something she refused to even consider.

Marriage. To Alek.

Twice within the same day that suggestion she marry had come at her. First from Jerry as a ridiculous solution to the problem with the immigration people, and now from her grandmother as the answer to her pain.

Julia stood, her arms cradling her middle. Glancing over at Ruth, she realized her grandmother was asleep. The grandmother who'd loved and supported her all her life, who'd stood by her when it seemed the whole world had exploded.

Julia remembered a time, long past, when she'd been a child and a fierce thunderstorm had raged in the dead of night. Terrified, she'd raced down the hallway to Ruth's room and slipped into bed with her. Even then she'd known that was the safest place in all the world for her to be.

That security had always been with her. Soon she would lose her anchor, the one who had guided and loved her. As best as she could remember, Ruth had never asked anything of her. Julia didn't know how she could refuse.

Julia's request came as little surprise. Aleksandr had been waiting for it since the scene in her office the day before. If he lived to be a wise, old man he doubted that he would ever understand this strange country he'd come to love. Nor was he likely to understand Julia

Conrad. She was a woman encased in frost, a woman with bruises on her soul. He'd recognized this from the moment they met. She was uncomfortable with him, he knew, from the way she avoided eye contact with him. He guessed subconsciously she recognized he'd seen through her mask and viewed her pain. He hadn't had much contact with her, and he suspected she avoided him, preferring to communicate through her brother.

Julia's secretary let him into the office and announced his arrival. Julia was sitting at her desk writing. When he entered the room, she glanced up and smiled.

"Please, sit down," she instructed with polite stiffness, motioning toward the chair on the other side of her desk. "I hope I'm not interrupting your work."

For a moment Aleksandr didn't trust himself to speak. Her pain was closer to the surface than before, almost visible beneath the thick facade she'd erected.

"I'm never too busy for you, Ms. Conrad," he acknowledged when he could, dipping his head slightly.

Her features seemed perfect to him, her beauty chilling, it was so flawless. He noted her creamy skin was flushed slightly, her eyes dark and clear as they studied him with equal interest.

"I thought it might be a good idea if we talked," she suggested haltingly.

He nodded. "About my work?"

She hesitated, and not answering, she stood and moved away from him, carefully placing herself, he noted, in the shadows where it was more difficult to read her expression.

"Tell me how your experiments are progressing," she instructed, her hands clenched behind her back. She resembled an attorney, pacing before the jury, one unsure of the strength of her case.

Aleksandr was well aware from the notes he received from her that Julia had read and understood his weekly reports. Nevertheless he humored her. The additives he'd been working on for Conrad paints had amazing capabilities. His first innovation had been a simple one. Once an exterior surface was painted, if the owner wished a different color at some later date, all that needed to be done was to wash the surface with another solution, one that would be available only through Conrad Industries. The idea had evolved into several areas, from homes to cars to lawn furniture.

His second innovation had been equally successful thus far. He'd developed a blend of chemicals that, when added to a surface, would promptly remove the old paint. No more scraping, or heating it away. A spray of the solution would dissolve it away with only a minimum of effort, without harmful effects or harsh chemicals to damage the environment.

Aleksandr gave Julia a detailed description of his experiments. It worried him that he wouldn't be with Conrad Industries to see his work come to fruition, but there was nothing more he could do. He felt regret to be leaving America, especially since there was such upheaval in his homeland.

He paused, awaiting her response.

"You're very close, then."

"Within a few months," he guessed.

Her delicate brows arched with what he suspected was surprise and delight. Both emotions quickly bled from her expression as she looked away. Her eyes avoided his and Aleksandr wondered privately at how many hearts she had broken. She held herself distant, the unattainable prize of many a man, the dream of loveliness. But untouchable and distant.

"Aleksandr." She said his name with a casual familiarity, although to the best of his knowledge it was the first time she'd addressed him personally. "We have a problem . . . as you know."

She moved toward him, her eyes wide and appealing, and when she spoke it was in a whisper. "We're too close to lose everything now. I can't let it happen. My brother offered a solution."

Aleksandr's mind churned with confusion, dulling his wits. She couldn't possibly be considering the suggestion they marry, could she? Only a day earlier she'd scoffed at her brother for even mentioning something so preposterous. Alek hadn't been given a chance to comment on the idea.

"I've given some thought to Jerry's suggestion," she continued demurely, glancing over her shoulder at him as she returned to her desk. "It seems marriage is our only solution."

Aleksandr wasn't fooled; there wasn't a shy, retiring bone in that delectable body of hers. Julia Conrad was too proud and stubborn to play the role well. There was no limit to her determination, and Aleksandr wasn't fooled.

"Naturally you'd be well compensated for your . . . contribution to Conrad Industries. Even more than we're currently paying you. We'd be happy to double your salary. Naturally it wouldn't be a real marriage, and when you've finished with your work, we'd obtain a quiet divorce. If you're agreeable, I'll have Jerry draw up a prenuptial agreement for us to sign."

Aleksandr was convinced if there'd been any other way to solve the problem, Julia would have opted for it. She was offering him a pretend marriage, followed by a discreet divorce.

He frowned, disliking that she'd opted to bribe him with money. His wages were already far beyond what he would ever hope to earn in Prushkin. His country was strangling itself on the wide range of opportunities sudden freedom had allotted. It seemed everything had to become much worse before democracy took root and the civil unrest quieted. The income he earned now, he mailed to his family, while he lived as frugally as possible himself.

"I understand there are several members of your family still in Prushkin," she said cautiously. "We might be able to help them immigrate to the States if we did decide to go ahead with the marriage."

At his continued silence, Julia added, "If that's something you'd care to consider... bringing your immediate family into the country. Is it?" she prompted.

Aleksandr's voice was strained when he spoke. "My sister is widowed and lives with my mother." Unable to remain seated, he stood and walked to the window, his back to her. He experienced a strong desire to take Julia into his arms, but he was painfully aware there was no warmth in her, nor would she welcome his touch.

For two years Aleksandr had studied Julia Conrad. She was as cold and intimidating as she was beautiful. It was a mask, one she wore well, but Alek knew better.

Outwardly she was often arrogant and sometimes sarcastic. But she wasn't capable of hiding her softer side from him. Every now and again he caught puzzling, contradictory glimpses of her. She deeply cared for her employees and was often generous to a fault. Then there'd been the day, shortly after Alek had come to America, when he'd seen Julia with her grandmother.

The facade had melted away from Julia that afternoon. If Alek hadn't seen it with his own eyes, he wouldn't have believed such a transformation was possible. Julia had glowed with joy and pride, giving her grandmother a tour of the rebuilt facilities. Alek had held the image of her that day in his mind ever since.

Marriage. He sighed inwardly. His religion didn't accept divorce and he refused to sacrifice his life and his happiness for a business proposition.

"I wish you'd say something," she said.

He returned to the chair and kept his features as expressionless as possible. "There's much we need to consider before we enter into this agreement."

"Of course," she returned.

"Your money does not interest me."

She seemed surprised by his words. "Even for your family?"

"Even for my family." What he earned now was adequate. Julia wasn't the only one who was proud. Alek couldn't be bought. She needed him, a woman who needed no one, and he appreciated what it had taken for her to approach him. Alek wasn't being completely unselfish, nor was he without greed. He already had a price set in his mind.

"Then what is it you want?"

He shrugged, not knowing how to tell her.

Restlessly she came to her feet, and walked away from him. He admired the smooth, fluid grace of her movements. She was a woman who moved with confidence, assured of herself and her surroundings. Usually. But at the moment she was sure of nothing and that disturbed her.

"I'm not sure what to say," Aleksandr answered truthfully.

"Do you find the idea of marriage to me so distasteful?" she asked.

"No," he assured her quietly. "You're quite lovely."

"Then what is it?"

"I don't want money."

"If it isn't money, then what is it? A percentage of my stock? A vice presidency in the company? Tell me." Her eyes were round and oddly appealing.

"You Americans regard marriage much differently than we do in Prushkin. In my country when a man and woman marry it is for many reasons, not all of them love. Nevertheless when we marry it is for life."

"But you aren't in Prushkin now, you're in America."

"Americans treat marriage like dirty laundry. When it becomes inconvenient, you toss it aside. My head tells me I live in your country now, but my heart believes in tradition. If we marry, Julia, and it would be my wish that we do, then there will be no divorce."

Her breath escaped in a rush and her dark eyes flared briefly.

Aleksandr ignored the fury he read in her and continued. "We both stand to gain from this arrangement. I will remain in the country and continue my experiments. You will have what you wish, as well. But there is a cost to this, one we should calculate now. The marriage will be a real one, or there will be no marriage."

Her gaze cut through him with ill-concealed contempt. "So you want more than the golden egg, you want the whole goose."

"The goose?" Aleksandr didn't know this story. He smiled. "In my country, goose is traditionally served for the wedding meal. I do not know about the golden egg, but you may keep that. I want only you."

Her voice was husky when she spoke. "That was what I thought."

The phone on her desk rang just then and Julia reached for it. "I said I didn't want to be disturbed," she said impatiently. Her features tightened and she blinked as she listened. "Yes, yes, of course, you did the right thing. Put me through immediately." A moment passed. "Dr. Silverman, this is Julia Conrad. I understand you've had my grandmother taken to Virginia Mason Hospital."

Alek waited and watched as the eyes that had been distressed and angry a moment earlier softened with stark emotion. She blinked and Alek thought he might have noticed the sheen of tears appear.

"Naturally. I'll let my brother know right away and we'll meet you there as soon as we possibly can. Thank you for contacting me so soon." She replaced the receiver, stood and started out of the room, apparently forgetting Aleksandr was there.

"Your grandmother is ill?" he asked.

She whirled around, seeming surprised at the sound of his voice, and nodded. "I... have to leave. I don't believe there's any need for us to discuss this matter further. I can't agree to your conditions. I refuse to be trapped in the type of marriage you're suggesting. I'd hoped we'd be able to work out some kind of compromise, but that doesn't seem possible."

"I'm disappointed. You would have given me several fine children."

She looked at him as if he'd spoken in his native tongue and she didn't understand a word he'd said. "Children?" she repeated softly, her voice dwindling. A sadness seemed to steel over her and she shook her head as if to dispel the image.

"I will think good things for your grandmother," Alek told her.

She nodded. "Thank you." With what looked like a hard-won poise, she turned and left the office.

Alek watched her go and the proud way in which she carried herself tugged at his heartstrings. He wished her grandmother well, but more important, he wished Julia a happy life.

Knowing his time in the States was limited to mere days, Aleksandr worked well past the time when his peers had left the laboratory. He felt it was his moral obligation to do everything within his power to see that the next series of experiments was performed to the standards and the conditions he'd set for the earlier ones. He wouldn't be with Conrad Industries to oversee the continued research, and that distressed him, but he had no choice.

The laboratory was silent and the sound of footsteps echoing down the wide corridor outside his office sounded like the rapid fire of a racquetball slammed against the side of the court.

He raised his eyes expectantly when Julia Conrad opened the door without knocking and walked inside.

She was pale, her eyes darker than he could remember seeing them.

"Julia," he said, standing abruptly. "Is something wrong?"

She stared at him as though she'd never seen him before. Looking around her, it seemed she didn't know where she was or how she got there.

"Your grandmother?" he guessed.

Julia nodded and gnawed on her bottom lip. "She . . . she suffered another heart attack."

"I'm sorry."

Her eyes flew upward as if to gauge the sincerity of his words. For a lengthy moment she said nothing. Then she inhaled a wobbly breath and bit into her lip with such vengeance Aleksandr feared she'd draw blood.

"I . . . I've reconsidered, Mr. Berinski. I'll marry you under the conditions you've set."

Chapter Two

"I don't want an elaborate wedding." Julia fussed, folding her arms around her middle, and moving to the far side of her office. Her brother was being impossible. "How could there possibly be time to arrange one?"

"Julia, you're not listening to me."

"I'm listening," she countered sharply. "I just don't happen to like what I'm hearing."

"A reception at the Four Seasons isn't so much to ask."

"But a wedding with guests and this whole thing with wearing a fancy wedding dress is ridiculous! Jerry, please, this farce is getting out of hand. I understand marriage is the best solution, but I didn't realize I was going to be forced to endure the mockery of a formal wedding."

Jerry gave a helpless gesture with his hands. "We've got to make this as credible as we can. Apparently you don't understand how important this charade is. It isn't just the wedding, either. That's only the first hurdle. You've got to make everything appear as though you're madly in love. Nothing less will convince the immigration people. If you fail...I don't even want to think about that."

"You've already gone through this." More times than she cared to count.

"Alek must live with you, too."

This was the part that disturbed Julia most. Her condo was her private haven where she could be herself. She was about to lose that, too. "But why?" She knew the answer, had argued and fussed until Jerry was blue with exasperation. Julia didn't blame him, but this marriage was becoming far more complicated than she ever thought it would.

"Why?" Jerry shouted, tossing his hands into the air. "I've made everything as plain as I can. Alek isn't the problem, it's you. What I don't understand, Julia, is why you're putting up such a fuss when we're the ones who stand to gain in this arrangement."

"You're making Alek sound like a saint for marrying me."

Jerry didn't answer right away, which irritated her all the more. "Let's put it this way," he said finally. "Conrad Industries is gaining far more from this union than Alek will ever see."

"I offered to pay him handsomely."

"You insulted him. The man has pride, Julia. He isn't doing this for the money."

"Then why has he agreed to go through with it?"

rugged. "The hell if I know."

rds reiterated that Alek wasn't getting any bargain marrying her. "He wants to help his family," Julia reminded her brother. She remembered Alek mentioning a widowed sister and his mother, even if Jerry didn't. As the oldest son, Alek would feel responsible for taking care of his family. Julia had promised to do whatever she could to bring both his mother and his sister to the United States. There were plenty of built-in incentives for Alek to go through with this marriage, enough for her not to concern herself about taking advantage of him.

"There's more to the man than meets the eye," Jerry insisted. "I'm convinced he's not interested in any monetary gain. When he read over the prenuptial agreement, he insisted on no interest in the company. We're about to make a fortune because of him, and he wants no part of it."

This discussion wasn't doing anything to ease Julia's conscience. "I agreed to the marriage," she reminded her brother, not wanting to stray any farther from the subject than they already had. "But no one said anything about a wedding. I thought we'd make an appointment with a justice of the peace and be done with it." She walked over to her desk, opened the lambskin appointment book and flipped through the pages. "Friday at four is open."

"Julia," Jerry returned with an exasperated sigh. "Don't be difficult. I've already explained—we've got to make this whole thing as real as we can for obvious reasons."

"I've agreed that Alek can move in with me." To Julia's way of thinking, that was a major concession.

She hadn't been thrilled about it, nor did she feel good about tricking Alek. He'd insisted from the first that their marriage be real. He made it known that he fully intended on sleeping with her, making love to her and to her amusement, impregnating her. Julia couldn't allow that. Alek didn't understand and neither did Jerry. Julia was incapable of love, the kind of trusting love a husband and wife shared. The ability was dead, destroyed by Roger's treachery. Never again would she put her faith in another man. Alek came to her fully expecting her to be his wife in every way. Soon he would learn the truth; soon he would know for himself how severely he was being cheated. Such deception didn't sit well with Julia, but there was no help for it.

While Julia admired Alek, she found herself nervous around him. He left her feeling naked and exposed. He seemed to be able to look into her very soul. Rationally she knew that was impossible, but she couldn't shake the suspicion that in some uncanny way he knew all there was to know about her.

"Immigration is going to ask about the wedding," Jerry continued. "We need positive proof that what prompted the marriage to Alek was nothing less than earth-shattering love. A hurried-up affair in some judge's chambers isn't going to work. They're going to want evidence of your commitment and devotion to each other."

"A hurried-up affair at the Four Seasons will convince them of all that?"

Jerry sighed once more. "It looks better. Now, I suggest you go out and get yourself a fancy wedding dress while I make the other arrangements with Virginia. We'll deal with the caterers and the photographers and see to having the invitations hand-delivered.''

"Jerry, this is crazy!" Julia protested. The idea of dressing up in an elaborate wedding gown, as if she were a loving bride on display, appalled her. Nor was she keen on being submitted to a series of photographs as though she were wildly and passionately in love with Alek. It was too much. "I can't go through with this," she said evenly.

"You've already agreed."

"To the marriage, yes, but not this...this circus. It's becoming a Hollywood production, a show for media attention."

"A show is what we need if we're going to fool the INS investigators," Jerry argued. "And trust me, Julia, this marriage will be investigated."

Julia walked over to the window and studied the street several floors below. In a moment of weakness, when her fears had been rampant and she was so deathly afraid of losing Ruth, Julia had gone to Alek and agreed to his terms. Even now she didn't understand what had prompted her. She was sick with analyzing it, furious with herself for being so weak. That morning, once her head was clear, she realized it had all been a mistake, but by then Alek had contacted Jerry, who'd put everything into motion. Now, it seemed, there was no turning back.

Her intercom hummed before Virginia's efficient voice reached out to her. "Mr. Berinski is here to see you."

Julia tossed a panicked look to her brother. She wasn't prepared to deal with Alek just yet. They hadn't spoken since she'd agreed to the marriage.

"Julia," Jerry prompted when she didn't respond.

"Send him in," Julia instructed her secretary, steeling herself for the confrontation.

No sooner had the words left her mouth when the door leading to her office opened. Alek walked in and the light in his dark eyes shone brightly as he gazed over at her. A slow, seductive smile worked its way over his lips.

"Good afternoon." Alek spoke to her brother first, then returned his attention to her. "Julia."

"Alek," she said briskly, surprised by how defensive she sounded.

He didn't seem the least taken back by her lack of welcome. The last time they'd spoken she'd agreed to become his wife, accepting the stipulations he'd set. She'd been overwrought with anxiety, she reasoned, frightened and lost. Yet no matter how hard she argued with herself, Julia realized she wouldn't change her mind...unless Alek wanted out.

"I was just clearing the wedding arrangements with Julia," Jerry explained.

Alek's eyes refused to leave Julia. She felt her face heat up with color and wished with everything in her that she could escape.

"I'd like some time alone with my intended," Alek requested.

Julia sent a pleading glance to her brother, not wanting him to leave her. Jerry ignored the unspoken request, mumbled something under his breath that she couldn't understand and walked out of the room.

"You want to talk?" she asked, putting on a brave front. She rubbed her palms together and walked away from him. Her shoulders felt stiff and her legs heavy.

"You're frightened?"

Terrified. Nervous. Afraid. None of those words adequately described what Julia was experiencing. The situation had an eerie, unreal quality to it that she couldn't shake. Only a few years earlier she'd looked forward to being a happy bride. She'd dreamed of the day that Roger would slip a wedding band onto her finger and look down on her with eyes filled with the strength of his love.

A flash of unexpected pain attacked her and she shook the image from her head.

"All brides are nervous," she said quietly in response to his question.

"How is your grandmother?"

"I'll be seeing her this afternoon ... better, I believe." According to the nurse Julia had spoken with that morning, Ruth had slept restfully through the night. But that had been after Jerry had spoken to her and explained that Julia would be marrying Aleksandr Berinski. To the best of her recollection, her grandmother had only met Alek once, and that had been recently. He'd apparently made quite an impression, because his name had cropped up with alarming frequency ever since.

"Do you wish to change your mind about the marriage?" Alek probed.

Her chance was here, handed to her on the proverbial silver platter. All she needed to do was explain that she hadn't been herself, that she hadn't been fully aware of what she was doing. She opened her mouth to explain it all away and found she couldn't. The words refused to come. Her throat refused to release them, and while she was fumbling for a reply, he moved behind her and rested his hands on her shoulders. He leaned forward and gently kissed the side of her neck.

Julia froze. It was the first time a man had touched her since Roger and her heart went into a panic. She was unable to move or breathe. Alek didn't seem to notice. He wrapped his arms around her middle and brought her back against him. His breath stirred shivers along her spine and a curious warmth crept into her blood.

Alek turned her around to face him. She wasn't given the opportunity to object as he pressed his mouth to hers. His lips were moist and parted as they moved slowly, seductively over hers. She wedged her hands between them, braced her palms against his hard chest and pushed herself free. Her lungs felt as though they would burst and she drew in a deep breath. The irony of it didn't escape her. His touch had been gentle, his kiss sweet and undemanding, and yet she'd felt as though she was suffocating.

Alek didn't seem offended or surprised by her actions. His eyes danced with mischief as they sought out hers. Julia raised the back of her hand to her mouth and pressed it there. She burned with anger. He'd done this intentionally so she'd know he expected to touch and kiss her often after the ceremony. She was to be his wife in every sense of the word and he wouldn't tolerate a loveless, sexless marriage. He wanted her and he was making damn sure she knew it.

Dear God, what was she going to do?

Julia stood outside the rental bridal shop with all the thrill and anticipation of a long overdue visit to the dentist.

She opened the door and stepped inside, grateful to notice the saleswoman wasn't overly busy.

"Hello."

"Hello," Julia said stiffly, fanning out the billowing chiffon skirt of a chartreuse bridesmaid dress which hung from the rack with a mild sense of distaste.

"May I help you?" came the friendly voice.

Julia revealed her lack of enthusiasm with a non-committal shrug. "I need a wedding dress for this Friday afternoon."

The shopkeeper was petite, Julia noticed, hardly more than five feet tall with soft sable brown hair. The woman was a dreamer; Julia could see it in her fawn brown eyes, She, too, had once worn that same look of hapless innocence, but that had long since been destroyed.

"The wedding is this Friday?"

"I know that doesn't give me much time, " Julia said, feeling foolish. "It's one of those spur-of-the-moment affairs."

"Don't worry," the saleswoman assured her, walking toward a long rack of plastic-covered wedding dresses. "Spur-of-the-moment weddings are often the most romantic."

Julia had nothing to add. One look told her the woman was more than a dreamer; she was also hopelessly sentimental. She was one of those who walked around with her head in the clouds when it came to love, and no doubt her attitude had been influenced by her job. She dealt with women who came to her when they were deeply in love and it seemed the entire world was their oyster.

Three years earlier, Julia had been just the same. Young, enthusiastic and so much in love that she didn't recognize what should have been obvious.

"I'd like a simple dress," she said forcefully, disrupting her thoughts. "Something plain."

"Plain," the woman repeated slowly.

"The plainer the better," Julia reiterated while she walked about the store.

"I'm afraid I have a limited selection of plain dresses."

That was what Julia feared. "Something simple, then."

"Simple and elegant?" she asked, grinning approvingly. "I have several. Would you like to sort through this rack? Choose the patterns that appeal to you, I'll write down the style and then you can try them on."

As far as Julia was concerned, this business with the wedding dress was a waste of precious time. She wanted it to be over and done with so she could head for the hospital and visit Ruth.

The saleswoman led the way to the appropriate display of gowns. Julia shuffled through them quickly, making two selections. Neither dress strongly appealed to her.

"I'll try on these two," Julia told the woman.

The woman made no comment as she journeyed into the back room and returned a few moments later with the two dresses in the appropriate size. She carried them into the dressing room and placed them on the hook.

Julia obediently followed her inside. She undressed and slipped into the first dress. It was just as the saleswoman had promised. Simple and elegant. A straight skirt made of the finest silk, a beaded yoke and cuffs. It looked fine, Julia guessed.

"No," the shop owner said with a good deal of certainty. "This one doesn't suit you."

"It looks..."

"No," the woman repeated. "Don't even bother to try on the next dress. It wouldn't suit you, either."

"Please, I don't have a lot of time."

"The dress is one of the most important aspects of your wedding. Every bride deserves to feel beautiful on her special day."

Julia didn't know why she felt like crying, but she did. Buckets of tears, whole fountains' worth welled up inside her. She was eternally grateful the woman didn't seem to notice. Brides deserved a whole lot more than feeling beautiful, they deserved to marry a man who loved them, too.

"Wait here," she instructed. She left the changing area and returned a few moments later, carrying a lovely ornate dress. The silk gown with pearls and sequins was anything but simple. Rarely had Julia seen any dress more intricate.

"Try it on," she requested when Julia hesitated.

"I...I don't think I should."

"Nonsense. This dress was designed for someone with your body type. It's perfect. It arrived this afternoon, almost as though I'd sent away for it with you in mind."

"I don't know." Still Julia hesitated. The woman held up the gown for her inspection. It was lovely, ten times more elaborate than the one she'd tried on earlier. Ten times more beautiful. It was the type of dress a much beloved bride would wear. One a woman in love would choose, knowing her groom would treasure her. A groom who would cherish her devotion all his life. It was the style of dress she would have worn for Roger before she learned of his betrayal. Before she'd learned what a fool she'd been.

She wanted to argue, but one look convinced her that the woman would hear none of it. Not exactly sure why she would allow this stranger to dictate her actions, Julia slipped into the elegant gown. The silk and taffeta rustled and hummed a low tune as it slid effortlessly over her hips. She kept her eyes lowered as she turned around and the shopkeeper fastened the small pearl closures down her back.

Julia felt strangely reluctant to look into a mirror, almost fearing her own reflection. When she did raise her eyes to the glass, she was startled at the beautiful young woman who gazed back at her. It took her a wild second to realize it was herself.

Gone were the lines that told of the bitterness and disappointment she'd carried with her like a heavy suitcase since her father's death. The cool, disinterested look in her eyes had warmed. The calculating side of her personality faded, replaced instead by the woman she'd been before she'd fallen in love with Roger Stanhope. The open, trusting soul, too young for her years, gullible and naive.

Unable to look at herself any longer, Julia dragged her eyes away from the graceful reflection of the woman she had once been. The one Roger Stanhope's deception had destroyed.

"It's perfect," the saleswoman was saying with a gentle sigh of appreciation. "Just perfect. It's as if the dress was meant for you."

Julia opened her mouth to contradict the store owner, but before she could voice her objection she looked to the mirror one last time. A few days earlier she'd happened to catch a stormy glimpse of herself reflected from her office window. She'd disliked what she'd seen, the woman she'd become, cold, uncaring, and driven.

The image had shaken her. She'd brushed aside her self-analysis, and had concentrated her efforts on what was happening with Alek and Jerry at the Immigration office instead. The events of that tempestuous afternoon had simmered down to this farce of a wedding.

Alek had been adamant that there be no divorce. Julia had agreed to those terms, but not in the spirit he'd intended. If it weren't for the circumstances involved in this arrangement, Julia sincerely doubted that she would ever have married. This would be her only wedding, her one chance to wear such a beautiful gown.

"I'll take it," she said, calling herself a fool even as she spoke.

"Somehow I knew you would," the saleswoman said, grinning broadly.

It took an additional forty minutes before Julia was able to leave the shop. Nervously she glanced at her watch as she headed toward her parked car. She was several minutes late and knew Ruth would be worried about her.

As often as she visited a hospital, Julia could never seem to accustom herself to the antiseptic smell. Her footsteps made abrupt clicking sounds as she rushed down the polished hallway to the wing that housed her grandmother. She hated the thought of Ruth being here, away from her comfortable home and her precious pictures she loved and kept close to her side.

Repeatedly Ruth had tried to prepare Julia for her death, but Julia refused to listen, refused to accept life without her dearest Ruth.

Checking in at the nurses' station, Julia was left to wait until the head nurse returned. A huge bouquet of red, blue, yellow and white flowers overfilled an inverted straw hat on the corner of the long counter. Julia had never seen a more striking arrangement. Within minutes Velma Williams, the head nurse, was back and Julia was ushered to Ruth's side.

"Good afternoon," Julia whispered, unable to tell if Ruth was sleeping or simply resting her eyes. Her grandmother seemed to be doing more of both lately. There were a variety of tubes and equipment attached to Ruth's body that monitored her heart and administered drugs intravenously. Julia looked down on this woman she loved so dearly and was forced to swallow back the growing sense of alarm. It seemed to ring in her ears like a school bell, announcing that the time was fast approaching when Ruth would no longer be with her.

The older woman's eyes gradually drifted open. "Julia, my dear, I'm so pleased you're here. Come sit with me."

Julia pulled up a chair and sat next to the high hospital bed. "How are you feeling?"

Ruth gestured weakly with her hand. "That's not important now. Tell me about you and Alek. How I've prayed for this day. How I've longed for you to release your pain and learn to love again."

"We're to be married this Friday afternoon." Julia half suspected her grandmother would find the immediacy of this wedding suspicious, but instead Ruth smiled tenderly and a faraway look came into her tired eyes.

"Friday... It's good that you won't have a long engagement, because I doubt I'll last much longer."

"Grandma, please don't say that. You're going to be around for years and years."

The weary smile didn't waver. "I'm going to miss seeing my great-grandchildren."

Julia wanted to argue with her, but there would never be children for her and Alek because there would never be a real marriage. She suffered a slight twinge of guilt but pushed the emotion aside. It was a luxury she couldn't afford.

"I'm sorry I'm late but I was trying on wedding dresses," Julia explained, forcing some enthusiasm into her voice. She was mildly surprised at how little effort it demanded to sound excited about the dress she'd found at the bridal shop. She described it in detail, and was pleased at the way her grandmother's eyes brightened.

"You and Alek will come see me after the ceremony, won't you?"

"Of course," Julia promised.

Ruth motioned toward the nurses' station. "He sent me flowers. He's such a thoughtful boy. Velma carried the bouquet in for me to see. Did you notice them?"

"Who sent you flowers?"

"Your Alek. An enchanting arrangement, and such a sweet thing to do. I like him, Julia, so very much. I have from the moment we met. You've chosen well, my dear."

Julia was uncomfortable talking about Alek. He'd been foremost in her thoughts all day and she wanted to escape him, escape the memory of his gentle kiss.

"Tell me all about your romance. You've been so closemouthed about it all . . . yet I knew." Ruth's eyes slowly closed and she sighed softly. With what seemed to require a good deal of effort she forced her eyes open. "He's a special man, that one. Just hearing about you two gladdens my heart."

"Ah . . ." Julia hesitated, not sure what to say. "It all happened rather quickly . . . almost overnight."

"So I gathered." A rare spark appeared in Ruth's eyes. "Oh, how I adore a love story. Tell me more before I grow too tired and drift off to sleep."

"Alek's green card was about to expire." Keeping everything as close to the truth as possible made this tale much easier.

"His green card," Ruth repeated. "Of course, I'd forgotten."

"He was going to have to return to Prushkin."

"That was when you realized you couldn't let that happen, wasn't it?"

"I hadn't realized how important he was to me," Julia said, sighing with a small bit of drama. "Jerry did everything he could to persuade the Immigration people to let Alek stay, but nothing he said convinced them. The three of us were talking and suddenly I realized how vital it was to me that Alek remain in the United States. I . . . don't think I could bear to go on without him." This was something of a stretch, but Julia knew what a romantic her grandmother was. If she was stretching the truth just a little, it was a small price to pay to satisfy Ruth's romantic heart.

"Julia, my sweet child." Her grandmother's delicate hand reached for Julia's and she squeezed her fingers. The pressure was shockingly weak. "I always trusted that in time you'd open your heart to love again. It took a special man like Alek. Be happy, my child. Promise me you won't let go until you've found your joy."

Julia wasn't sure she understood Ruth's words. They made little sense to her. She would have quizzed her if Ruth hadn't chosen that moment to slip into a peaceful slumber. For several moments Julia remained at her grandmother's side, soaking in the solace she felt whenever she spent time with Ruth.

"Julia." The sound of her name, said with that soft European accent, snatched her attention. She jerked around to find Alek's presence filling the doorway.

She stood abruptly, resenting his intrusion into these quiet moments. She walked toward the door, not wanting him to interrupt her grandmother's rest.

"What are you doing here?" she asked when they were well into the corridor.

He lifted the edge of his mouth in a half smile. "I came to see you. There is much we need to decide." He tucked her hand in the crook of his elbow and sauntered toward the elevator.

"I left the arrangements for the wedding in Jerry's hands. He'll arrange everything. As far as I can see, there's nothing to discuss."

She witnessed the anger in him, in the prideful square of his shoulders, and the way his mouth thinned and his eyes snapped.

"You want me, Julia, you need me. I just wonder how long it will take before you realize this."

The arrogance of the man was beyond description. She glared at him, wanting to make him eat his words. She needed no one, especially a man, and never a husband. She longed to shout out the truth, but couldn't.

Long seconds passed and electricity arced between them.

"You need me."

"You're wrong," she returned defiantly. Conrad Industries needed him, but she didn't.

Their eyes lingered and it seemed neither of them knew what to say or do next. Jerry had mentioned to her how proud Alek was, and she saw that colossal ego for herself. He released her arm from his elbow and turned away.

He was halfway down the hospital corridor when Julia spoke.

"I'm not willing to admit I need you, Alek," she called after him. She had to say something. They would quickly make each other miserable if this friction between them continued. If he wasn't willing to make an effort, then it was up to her.

"So you've already said."

"But I am willing to admit we need each other."

Grinning, he turned back. His smile grew as he returned to her side. For the span of an uneven heartbeat, he said nothing. Then he lowered his mouth to hers and gently kissed her. As before, his touch was as soft as a kitten's fur, as light as air, leaving her to wonder if she'd imagined his kiss.

"What was that for?" she asked, gazing up at him.

His smile was worth waiting for. "Because, my soon-to-be-wife, you deserved it." He brushed the hair from her temple. "For that matter," he said with a roguish grin, "so did I."

Chapter Three

The wedding ceremony was a nightmare for Julia. When it came time for her to repeat her vows, her throat closed up and she was barely able to speak. Not so with Alek. His voice rang out loud and clear, without the least hesitation.

Love and cherish.

Julia's conscience was screaming. She had no intention of loving Alek. She didn't want to love any man, because love had the power to hurt her, the power to break her. Julia had worked hard to blot the emotion from her life. She could live without it. Love was superfluous, unnecessary, painful when abused, and her tender heart had yet to recover from her first bout.

Signing the final documents was even worse than having to endure the mockery of a ceremony. Her hand trembled as she wrote out her name on the marriage certificate. Her eyes glazed with tears as she stared at the official document, all too aware of the lie she was living.

Jerry, her secretary and the minister all seemed heedless of her distress. She didn't know what Alek was thinking. His fingers pressed gently against the small of her back as though to encourage her. Her hand continued to hold the pen and she remained bent over the document long after she'd finished signing her name.

"May your marriage be a long and fruitful one," the minister was saying to Alek. Julia squeezed her eyes closed, drew in a steadying breath and straightened. She dared not look to Alek for fear he could read her thoughts.

Long and fruitful, Julia's mind echoed. A sob welled inside her and she thought she might burst into tears. This deception was so much more difficult than she'd ever imagined.

"Shall we join the others?" Jerry, who had served as Alek's best man, suggested, gesturing toward the door. Julia was grateful for an excuse to leave the room.

The reception was held in a large hotel suite across the hall from where the wedding had taken place. Their guests were helping themselves to a wide variety of hors d'oeuvres served on silver platters, and crystal flutes of champagne.

Julia was surprised by how many people had come on so short a notice. Most were business associates, but several family friends were also in attendance. She had few friends left, allowing the majority of relationships to lapse after her father's death.

Alek was at her side, smiling and cordially greeting their guests. He placed his arm casually around her shoulders with unwelcome familiarity. Julia stiffened at his touch, but if he noted her uneasiness, he paid no heed.

"Have I told you how beautiful you look?" he whispered close to her ear.

Julia nodded. He hadn't been able to take his eyes off her from the moment she'd arrived in the wedding dress. Oddly, that depressed her, planning to deceive him the way she was. He was expecting much more from this union than she ever planned to give him. It would have been far better had she opted for the plain, simple, unattractive dress instead of the ornate one she'd chosen.

The minute she viewed herself in the dress before the wedding, she was sorry she'd ever agreed to this particular one. Even Jerry had seemed dumbstruck when he went to escort her to Alek's side. He'd become especially maudlin with his compliments, which added to her stress. And her guilt.

"Could you pretend to love me?" Alek whispered close to her ear. "Just for these few hours?" His warm breath against her skin sent shivers down her spine. "Smile, my love."

She obediently complied, her lips freezing with the motion.

"Better," he murmured under his breath.

"How soon before we can leave?"

Alek chuckled softly. "I know you're anxious for me, but if we left so soon, it would be unseemly."

Julia's face burned with a wild blush, which appeared to amuse Alek all the more. "Would you like me to get you a plate?" he offered.

She shook her head. Food held no appeal. "Do you want something?"

He turned to her, his eyes ablaze. "Rest assured, I do, but I'll collect my dessert later."

Julia's knees felt as though they wouldn't support her much longer. From obligation more than desire, she drank a glass of champagne. It must have been more potent than she realized because she felt giddy and light-headed afterward.

It was the dress, she decided. She wanted out of the wedding gown because it made her feel things she had no right to experience. With Alek standing at her side, she felt beautiful and wanted and loved when she didn't deserve or want any of it. She'd gone into this marriage for all the wrong reasons. She was uncomfortable, duping Alek the way she was. Using him for her own gain, giving nothing of herself in return.

Until she'd stood before the preacher, marriage had been little more than a word, part of the English language. She hadn't expected a few words mumbled before a man of God to be so powerful. Julia had been wrong. She was left shaken and uncertain in the aftermath, as if she was mocking basic human values.

"Jerry." With near desperation, she reached out to her brother and clasped his arm with both hands. "I've got to get out of here...."

He must have read the desperation in her eyes, because he nodded gravely. Whatever he said to Alek, Julia didn't hear. She assumed her brother would lead her from the room, but it was Alek who wrapped his arm around her middle. It was her husband who led her out of the reception.

"Jerry is making our excuses," he explained.

She nodded. "I'm sorry," she whispered as he led her down the hallway to the changing room. "I don't know what happened."

"Are you faint?"

"I'm fine now, thanks." She would be, when she was out of this dress and into her own clothes. She'd feel much better once he removed his arm from her waist. The walls had seemed to close in around her. She wished Alek would leave her, but he stayed even when she reached the door leading to the changing room.

"We didn't kiss," Alek whispered.

Julia didn't bother to pretend what he was talking about. When it came time for Alek to kiss his bride, Julia had made certain he'd gotten little more than a peck on the cheek. Alek had been disappointed, and Jerry's eyes had revealed his frustrated dissatisfaction. The lusty kiss would have put a seal on their act.

"You're not sick, are you?"

She could have lied, could have listed countless excuses, but she didn't. "I'm fine."

"Then I'll kiss my bride."

Her first instinct was to put him off, to thwart him as she had earlier and as she intended to later, but a kiss seemed like such a small price to pay to ease her conscience. His touch had always been tender, as if he understood and appreciated her need for gentleness.

"Yes," she agreed breathlessly.

Her back was against the wall and his arms slipped around her waist. Unsure of what to do with her own hands, she splayed them across his chest. He pulled her close and for a long moment held her, as if savoring the feel of her in his arms.

The trembling returned and Julia closed her eyes. She could smell his male-scented cologne, feel his heart beat beneath her flattened palms. His breath echoed in her ears, and rustled her hair.

His mouth met hers. His touch was light and brief, the way a morning mist caresses the petals of an opening rose. She tipped her head back and her eyes, of their own accord, drifted closed. His mouth brushed hers again. And again. A sigh worked its way through her as his tongue outlined the shape of her mouth. Leisurely he took a long series of nibbling kisses before catching her lower lip gently between his teeth and sucking.

Julia held her breath, unable to respond. She was content to let him be the aggressor, to allow him to taste and sample her without fully participating herself.

For a long moment her lack of involvement satisfied Alek. His mouth grazed over hers, circled and nibbled.

"Julia," he pleaded, "kiss me back."

Tentatively, shyly, her mouth opened to him and he moaned as though she'd greatly pleased him, and deepened the kiss. His arms tightened their hold and he hungrily slanted his mouth over hers. Strange, unwelcome pleasure rippled down her body as he moved against her. Even through several layers of silk and taffeta, Julia was aware of his desire for her.

Against every dictate of her will, she sighed at the rush of sensation she experienced. She felt hot and shaky, as though she'd suffered a near miss, as though she'd stepped off a curb and felt the rush of a car pass and had been inches from being struck. With the fear came a keen excitement that sang through her blood. A melody as ancient as time, the song of desire, of physical need and fulfillment. The two feelings collided, making her daring and impatient. She tilted her head back and welcomed the exploration of his tongue into her mouth. His movements were hot and greedy, insatiable, touching her in bold, intimate ways.

Her hands, which had seemed so useless moments before, were busy ruffling through his dark hair. Her body, so long barren, so long untouched, felt as if it were about to explode. She moved against him, clinging to him, fighting back tears.

The sound of someone clearing his throat broke the spell. Alek stilled, as did Julia. Slowly, reluctantly, she opened her eyes to find half the reception lined up outside in the hall watching them.

Jerry stood in the background, smiling broadly. He gave her a thumbs-up sign, looking ecstatic with glee. If they were looking to fool their guests, they'd succeeded beyond her brother's expectations.

As though loath to do it, Alek released her. He seemed perturbed by the interruption and growled something in his native tongue.

"I'll change clothes," she said, hurriedly moving into the room. She was grateful a chair was there. Sinking onto the cushion, she pressed her hands to her red face and closed her eyes. She felt as if she'd leaped off a precipice in the dark and had no idea of where she'd be landing. What had started out as a kiss had become something much more. She had been looking to soothe her conscience, but instead had added to her growing list of offenses, leading Alek to believe he should expect more.

Julia took her time changing her clothes. Twenty minutes later she reappeared in a bright red flowered dress she'd found in the back of her closet. These days she dressed mostly in business suits. Jackets, straight skirts and plain white blouses made up the majority of her wardrobe. The dress was a leftover from her college days. The design was simple and stylish.

Alek was pacing the hallway and appeared to be anxiously waiting for her.

"I'm sorry I took so long."

His smile was enthusiastic. He reached out and touched her lips. They remained sweetly swollen from his kiss, she realized. The color hadn't faded from her cheeks, either; if anything, it had deepened with this fresh appraisal.

"I . . . promised my grandmother we'd stop in at the hospital after the reception," Julia said nervously. "I'd hate to disappoint her."

"By all means we will see her."

Julia knew the minute they walked into the hospital room that Ruth had been waiting for them. Her grandmother's smile was wide and filled with a wealth of love as she held her hands out to them.

Julia rushed forward and gently hugged this woman she loved so dearly. It was clear each and every time she was with her grandmother that Ruth was close to death. She clung to life, not for herself, but for Julia's sake. It hurt her to know Ruth was in pain. Why were those who were good always the ones to suffer? Why couldn't God spare her grandmother for just a few more years? This day, her wedding day, seemed to have caused a caldron of emotions to churn and pop to the surface of her mind. She couldn't bear to think of what her life would be like without her grandmother.

It had been Ruth's gentle kindness that had gotten her through Roger's deception and her father's death.

Otherwise, Julia feared she would have ended up in a mental ward.

Emotions long buried and ignored arrived unexpectedly, as well. Kissing Alek had opened a storehouse of needs she had assumed were lost to her.

There were no answers for her, at least none she felt confident enough to face. Only myriad questions that assailed her from every front. She couldn't trust herself; her power to discern had been sadly lacking once and had cost her and her family dearly. She dared not trust herself a second time.

She was married to a man she didn't love and who didn't love her. To complicate everything, her grandmother was dying. This was what her life had boiled down to. A loveless marriage and a desperate loneliness.

Julia closed her eyes. She sought no answers and yet they'd come unbidden to her. She found them to be even more painful than the questions. They stripped away her strength and left her vulnerable and detached.

When Julia released her grandmother, Ruth looked up at her and brushed the tears from Julia's cheeks. "Tears?" she asked softly. "This should be the happiest day of your life."

Alek placed his arm around Julia's waist and helped her into the chair next to the bed. He stood behind her, his hands cupping her shoulders. His touch was light and tender. Julia pressed Ruth's hand to her cheek and held it there. Her grandmother looked much weaker this day, paler.

"I remember the day I married Louis," she said with a wistful smile.

Her grandfather had been dead many years now. The man was only a fuzzy memory to Julia, who guessed she'd been about seven or eight when he died.

"I was frightened out of my wits."

"Frightened?" Julia didn't understand.

"I wondered if I was doing the right thing. There were very few divorces in those days and if a woman happened to marry the wrong man, she was often sentenced to a miserable life."

"But you'd known him for a long time, I thought."

Ruth arched one delicate brow. "A long time?" she repeated with a lofty smile. "In a manner of speaking, you're right. But in reality we'd only gone out for a handful of dates before we married."

"I'd always assumed you knew Grandpa for years."

Ruth's hand stroked Julia's cheek. "It's true that in the early days Louis worked for my father. I'd see him now and again when I stopped in at the office, but those times were rare."

Julia was enthralled. She knew her grandmother had deeply loved her grandfather, but she couldn't remember ever hearing the story of their courtship.

"Then when did you happen to fall in love?"

"Louis quit working for my father, and Dad was furious with him. They were both strong-willed men and it seemed they were constantly butting heads. Louis started his own business in direct competition to my family." She closed her eyes and smiled whimsically. "It was a bold move in those depression years, before the war. He managed to hold his head above water, which infuriated my father even more. I think Dad would have taken a good deal of pleasure in seeing Louis fail." She paused in her narration and briefly closed her eyes as though to gather her strength. "Then the war came and Louis joined the army in what young people today call Special Forces.

"Before he left for England he stopped off at the house. I thought he was there to see my father. Can you imagine my surprise when he assured me I was the one he'd come to see? He told me he was going overseas and he asked if I'd be willing to write him. Naturally I told him I would be, and then he did the strangest thing."

When Ruth didn't immediately continue, Julia prompted her. "What did he do?"

Ruth gently shook her head. "It was such a little thing and so very sweet, so very much like Louis. He reached for my hand and kissed it."

Her grandmother's gaze fell to her hand, as if she felt it still.

"As I look back on that moment all those years ago," Ruth went on, "I realize it was then that I lost my heart to Louis. You see, I don't believe he ever expected to return from the war. He loved me then, he told me much later, and had for a very long time, but my father was a rich man and Louis feared Dad would never approve of him."

"How long was he away?"

"I didn't see him for three years, although I heard from him regularly. I treasured his letters and read them so many times I nearly wore them out. By the time he returned home I was so deeply in love with him, nothing else mattered. My family knew how I felt and I feared the worst when Dad insisted on accompanying me when I met Louis's train."

"What happened?"

Ruth's smile was weak, but happy. "Dad offered him his old job back. Louis accepted and almost immediately asked me to be his wife. I agreed and we were married less than a month later."

"What a beautiful story."

"We had a wonderful life together, better than I dared dream. I miss him still."

Julia knew her grandmother had taken Louis's death hard. For a long while afterward she'd closed herself off from life. It was in those bleak times that Julia's father had wisely sent Julia and Jerry to spend the summers with their grandmother.

"You, my children," Ruth continued, looking to Alek, "will have a good life, too. Alek, be gentle with my lamb. Her heart's been bruised, and she can be prickly, but all she needs is love and patience."

"Grandma!"

Ruth chuckled and gestured with her hand. "Off with you now. You don't want to spend your wedding night with me."

"I love you," Julia whispered as Ruth settled back against the pillows. "Rest easy and I'll call you in the morning."

"It was a rare pleasure to spend this time with you," Alek said. Reaching for her grandmother's hand, he bent down and kissed it. "I would have liked your Louis," he told her. "He was a rare man of honor."

A smile coaxed the corner of Ruth's mouth. "Indeed he was. When we first married, there was talk, there always seemed to be talk. Some folks said Louis had married me for my connections, for the money I would one day inherit. Few realized the truth. I was the fortunate one to have such a man love me."

Julia looked to Alek and when their eyes met, she quickly looked away.

"Now go," Ruth urged. "This is your wedding night."

The words echoed in Julia's ears like a huge Chinese gong. Her grandfather had been a man of honor, but she hadn't inherited his grit or his honesty. She planned to cheat Alek and he was about to discover exactly how much.

Julia had surprised him. Alek had misjudged this woman who was now his wife. For two years he had studied her, amazed at her tenacity. Jerry had told him little of what had led to the company's financial problems. Ever since his arrival, he'd learned bits and snatches of what had happened, but no one had sat down with him and explained the events that had led to near financial ruin. From what he understood, Conrad Industries had come very close to introducing a long-lasting exterior paint. One with a twenty-five-year guarantee. It seemed the company was on the brink of making one of the most innovative and progressive advances in the industry. This latest high-tech development was sure to have a dynamic impact on sales and give Conrad Industries a badly needed financial boost. The company had been set for expansion, confident of success. It was then that a series of mishaps occurred.

This was the part that remained vague to Alek. There'd been some sort of scandal having to do with another product produced by the company. A government recall, although Alek wasn't sure what that entailed. He'd heard something about a burglary, too. But by far the worst was a huge fire that had destroyed the laboratory and the warehouse. Not until much later had they learned the fire had been arson.

An employee was suspected. That much he'd learned from Jerry. But there wasn't enough proof to prosecute whoever it had been. Shortly after the fire, Jerry and Julia's father had suffered a heart attack and died. It was then that Julia had taken over the company. They'd struggled for a year before Jerry made the arrangements to bring Alek over from Prushkin. Since that time he'd been working hard on implementing his ideas.

"You're very quiet," Julia commented, breaking into his thoughts.

He glanced over at his bride. Her nervousness didn't escape him. He wished to do whatever necessary to put her at ease. He'd enjoyed listening to the story of Ruth and Louis Conrad's love. It had touched his heart, reminding him of his own grandparents, long dead. They'd deeply loved each other and he could have asked for no finer heritage. His grandfather had died first and his grandmother had followed less than a year later. His mother claimed her mother-in-law had perished from a broken heart.

Julia shifted restlessly in the car seat. He caught the movement from the corner of his eye, and wondered about this woman who had captured his heart. He knew the instant Jerry had suggested they marry that he would accept nothing less than total commitment from her. He was not a man who did things by half measure. He looked forward to the time he would bed his wife. He'd sensed fire in her, but hadn't realized how hot the flames had fanned until they'd kissed. Really kissed.

No woman had ever affected him as strongly as Julia. The kisses had enhanced his appetite for what was to follow. He would be patient with her. Gentle and slow. Although every instinct insisted he take her to his bed now, do away with her fretting and worry so they could enjoy the rest of the evening together. He must be patient, he reminded himself.

"Where would you like to go for dinner?" he asked. He suggested a couple of his favorite restaurants.

"Dinner?" she echoed, as though she'd hadn't given the matter a second thought. "I . . . don't know."

"You decide."

"Would you mind if we went to my . . . our condo?"

Alek's nod was eager. Her choice was a stroke of genius. She would relax there and—what was the American term—unwind? Yes, she would unwind for him so that when the time came for them to retreat to the bedroom, she would be warm with wine and eager for his touch.

"We'll have to send out for something," Julia announced when they reached the high-rise condominium. It was situated in the heart of downtown Seattle on the tenth floor, overlooking Puget Sound. A white-and-green ferry could be seen in the distance. The jagged peaks of the Olympic Mountains rose majestically to the west. The day had been clear and bright. Now the sun was setting, casting a pink glow over the scenery.

"Send out?" he repeated, frowning.

Julia stood in the middle of her modern home and clenched her hands in front of her. She resembled a disobedient child. "I don't cook much."

"Ah." Now he understood. "I am excellent in the kitchen." In the bedroom, too, but he couldn't say that without embarrassing her. She would learn that soon enough.

"You want to cook our dinner?"

"Yes," he answered, pulling his attention from the wide, strongly appealing view and following her into the kitchen. He liked her home. There was nothing so luxurious in Prushkin with which to compare it. The living room was long and narrow with windows that extended the full length of the condominium. The dining room and kitchen were both compact, as if their importance was minimal.

"Would you like a glass of white wine?" Julia asked him.

"Please." While she was busy with the wine, he explored his new home. A narrow hallway led to two bedrooms. The larger was dominated by a king-size bed, covered with a thick bright blue comforter and what seemed like a hundred small pillows. The scent of flowers, violets he guessed, hung in the air. The second bedroom was much smaller and the closet was filled with boxes. A quick examination revealed Christmas decorations.

He returned to the kitchen and took the wineglass from his wife's hand. Her eyes, so dark and round, appealed to him, but for what he wasn't sure. One thing was certain, Alek knew he couldn't wait much longer to make love to her.

Julia felt like a long-tailed fox about to be released for the hunt. She would soon be trapped. Alek didn't realize, at least not yet, that she had no intention of sleeping with him. Thus far he'd been kind, patient and gentle, but she couldn't count on his goodwill lasting much longer.

"I found a couple of chicken breasts in the freezer," she told him. It felt as though she were in danger of swallowing her heart. She was pretending for everything she was worth, acting out the role of the devoted wife, when she was anything but. "I'll make the salad."

He was searching through her drawers, stopping when he came across an old cloth dish towel. He tucked it at his waist and continued to survey her cupboards, bringing down a series of ingredients.

He started to hum as he worked. He'd chopped an onion, green pepper and several mushrooms by the time she scooted a stool to the counter. Perhaps she'd learn something. She had often seen Alek working in the laboratory. But now he amazed her with the familiar way he worked around her kitchen, as if this was truly his second home.

"When did you learn to cook?"

"As a boy. My mother insisted and I enjoy it."

"Thank her for me."

Alek paused and, glancing her way, smiled. "You can do that yourself someday. I'm doing what I can now to arrange for her arrival in the States."

"If...there's anything I can do, please let me know."

He nodded, seemingly pleased by her offer.

Julia drank her wine and refilled both their glasses. Her mind was working at a frantic pace, devising ways of delaying the inevitable moment when he'd learn the truth. Her original plan had been to get him drunk. Two glasses of wine and already she was feeling light-headed and a bit tipsy. Alek had consumed the same amount and was as sober as a nun. He wielded a large knife like a baton without the slightest hesitation.

Her second thought was to appeal to his sense of honor. A strange tactic, she admitted, coming from a woman who planned on cheating him out of his husbandly rights. He must realize she didn't love him. This was a business arrangement that profited them both. Making something personal out of it could ruin everything.

The kiss. Dear God in heaven, she must have been mad to allow him to kiss her the way he had. She'd done nothing to resist him. Instead she'd encouraged him, led him to believe she welcomed his touch.

She'd been left shaken in the aftermath, trying to summon some reason from the chaos in her mind. It shouldn't have happened. The very fact she'd allowed him to hold her and touch her in such an intimate manner defeated her purpose. Anger rose within her, not at Alek, but with herself for having allowed matters to go so far. Now Alek expected more, much more, and she couldn't, wouldn't allow it. She was angry, too, with the enjoyment she'd found in his arms. It shook her even now. It was as if she'd been looking for a way to prove herself as a woman, to show him and others that she was more feminine than anyone ever suspected.

Her childish foolishness had complicated everything.

"More wine?" she asked in a fit of nerves. The rice was cooking in a covered pot and the chicken was simmering in a delicious sauce. The aroma filled the kitchen. Alek was humming, looking relaxed and at ease while Julia calculated how many steps it would take to reach the front door.

Alek shook his head. "No more wine for me."

"I'll set the table," she offered, scooting down off the stool and moving into the dining room. Soon he would know. Soon he would discover what a phony she was. Her gaze sought the door once more. A coward. That was what she was. But the fault seemed almost minor when added to her previous sins. She was a liar and a cheat and now a coward.

Her hands were trembling as she set the silverware on the table. She added water glasses, anything to delay her return to the kitchen. Her return to Alek.

Alek had dished up their plates when she strolled back into the room. Julia didn't know if it was possible for her to down a single bite and she watched transfixed as he carried their meal into the dining room.

"Julia, my love."

"I'm not your love," she told him coolly, pressing herself back against the kitchen counter.

His grin was slow and easy. Undisturbed. "Not yet, perhaps, but you will be soon."

A fly, that was what she was, trapped in a spindly web awaiting her merciless fate. She closed her eyes, fearing that in his anger he might force her.

"Come, let us eat," Alek said, taking her unresisting hand and leading her to a chair. With impeccable manners, he held it out for her, then seated himself.

"This is very nice," she said. The smells were heavenly. In other circumstances she would have appreciated his culinary skills.

"My sister is an excellent cook," he announced casually. He removed the linen napkin from the table and spread it across his lap. "If you agree, she will prepare our meals once she arrives from Prushkin. She'll welcome the job and it'll simplify her receiving a visa."

"Of course..." Julia was more than willing to be generous with his family. For obvious reasons.

"You are nervous?" Alek asked, after sampling several bites. Julia hadn't managed even one taste.

"Yes."

He grinned. "Understandably so. Don't worry, my lamb, I will be gentle with you."

Julia's heart plummeted.

"I admire you, Julia. It isn't any woman who would accept the terms of our marriage. You are brave as well as very beautiful. I feel fortunate to have married such a fine woman."

Chapter Four

Julia vaulted to her feet, startling Alek. Her hand clenched the pink linen napkin as though it were a lifeline, and her sweet, dark eyes filled with tears.

"Julia?"

"I can't do it. I can't go through with it . . . you expect me to share your bed and for us to live like a normal married couple, but I just can't do it. I lied . . . everything's a lie. I'm sorry, Alek, truly sorry."

"You agreed to my terms," he reminded her without rancor. She was pale and trembling and it disturbed him to see her in such emotional torment. He would have liked to take her in his arms and comfort her, but he could see she wouldn't welcome his touch.

"I was overwrought. I . . . I didn't know what I was doing. Everything happened so fast."

Alek tested her words and, disagreeing, slowly shook his head. "You knew."

She retreated a couple of steps. "I've had a change of heart. It's understandable, given the circumstances."

It pained him to see her so distraught, but she'd willingly agreed to his stipulations, and there had been ample opportunity for her to speak her mind before the wedding. Calmly he reminded her of this.

"You didn't have to go through with the ceremony, but you did," he said. "You wanted this marriage, but refuse to admit it even to yourself." He stared at her, demanding that she relent and recognize her foolishness. They were married, the deed was done and she was his wife. There was no going back now.

"I . . . I was emotionally trapped. Jerry was convinced marrying you was the only way to keep you in the country. My grandmother is dying and she likes you, believes in you, and it seemed, I don't know, it just felt like the right thing to do at the time."

"It doesn't feel right now?" he asked, quelling his mounting frustration with her.

"No," she stated emphatically. "It doesn't feel the least bit right."

Alek rubbed his hand over his chin as he contemplated her words. "You Americans have many sayings I do not understand. You use much slang. There is one bit I remember and it seems to fit this situation."

"What's that?"

"Hogwash."

Julia went speechless and pale. Once she'd composed herself, she tilted her head at a regal angle and glared at him with open defiance. Alek suspected she used this cold, haughty regard to intimidate those who dared to differ with her. A mere look was incapable of daunting him from his purpose. It was apparent his bride had much to learn about him.

"Have you so little pride," she asked disdainfully, "that you would hold me to an agreement made when I was emotionally and physically distraught?"

Alek was impressed with her ability to twist an argument. "Pride," he echoed slowly, as if tasting the full flavor of the word. "I am a proud man. But what are you, Julia? Have you so little honor that you would renege on an agreement made in good faith and expect me to accept weak excuses?"

Her face reddened and she slumped into her chair.

"I've fulfilled my part of the bargain," he continued. "Is it wrong or unjust to expect you to live up to yours? I think not. You have what you wanted, what you needed. Is it not right that you satisfy my meager demands?"

She glared at him and even though an entire room separated them, Alek could feel the heat of her outrage. "You ask too much."

"All I ask is that you be my wife—share my life, and bear my children."

A trail of tears marked her pale cheeks. "You have every right to be angry, every right to curse me, but I can't be your wife the way you want."

"It's too late to change your mind." His voice was flat and hard. "We are married. You spoke your vows, you signed your name to the document. There is no turning back now. I suggest you forget this foolishness and finish your meal."

"Please try to understand. This isn't easy for me, either, I've been sick with guilt. I don't want to cheat you ... I never wanted that."

Alek sighed, his patience shrinking. "You're beginning to sound like a disobedient child."

"You're right about one thing," she said, gesturing beseechingly with her hands. "I should have said something sooner, I should never have gone through with the ceremony, but it's not too late. I'm saying something now."

"We are married." He sat down at the table and reached for his fork. He refused to give her the satisfaction of thinking her arguments had troubled him.

In abject frustration, Julia tossed her arms into the air. "You're impossible."

"Perhaps," he agreed readily enough. "But you are my wife and you shall remain so."

She bit back a retort, and seeing the effort it cost her amused him. Not another moment passed before she stormed out of the dining room. He heard her in the kitchen banging around pots and pans, but couldn't be sure of what she was doing. He finished each bite of his meal, although his appetite had long since left him.

Apparently she tried to make a phone call, but whoever she called hadn't answered. From his chair he witnessed her frustration when he saw her replace the receiver and press her forehead against the wall phone.

When he'd finished his dinner, Alek returned to the kitchen to find Julia busily rinsing dishes and placing them inside the dishwasher.

She ignored him for several moments, until he said, "Shall we ready ourselves for bed?"

Julia froze, then turned and stared at him. The shocked look she wore produced a surge of pride. "Are you mad?" Each word was spoken slowly, as if he didn't yet understand English.

"No," he answered thoughtfully. "I am a husband. Yours."

"I'm sorry, Alek," she said, her face pale, her voice shaking. "I should have said something before the ceremony... I've put a call in to my brother. As soon as possible I'll make whatever arrangements are necessary to have our marriage annulled."

Alek didn't swallow the bait. Jerry Conrad was his friend, and had sanctioned this marriage with his sister. The attorney had been the one to suggest it and had encouraged the union from the beginning.

Although Jerry hadn't shared his concerns with Alek, he was convinced Julia's brother was worried about his sister. Whenever Jerry mentioned Julia's name his eyes would cloud. After working with her these past two years, Alek understood her brother's anxieties. She was aggressive, domineering and driven. Of themselves those attributes weren't negative, especially for a woman involved in a competitive business, but Alek had noticed something more. Julia Conrad had closed off her life from everything that didn't involve Conrad Industries. Perhaps he was a fool, but Alek saw this ice-encased woman as a challenge. He liked Julia and with very little encouragement he could find himself deeply in love with her. Already he admired her and he longed for the day that he could cherish her love.

No, Alek reasoned, Jerry wouldn't give in to her dictates. He would be unemotional and reasonable. He couldn't count on the same behavior from Julia. Smiling to himself, he decided he rather looked forward to the contest of wills.

Alek had met Jerry years earlier while the young American had toured the European continent. Together they'd spent a restless day in a train station. Eager to learn what he could of America, Alek had questioned the student and found they shared several interests. Alek had liked Jerry. They had corresponded over the years and Alek had shared with his American friend his frustration with his country and his work. Jerry had offered Alek employment soon after the fire had nearly destroyed Conrad Industries. It had taken them almost a year to secure the necessary arrangements for him to live in the United States.

"Do you understand what I'm saying?" Julia asked. "I'm arranging an annulment."

"Yes, my love."

"I am not your love," she cried, sounding close to tears.

"Perhaps not now," he returned with supreme confidence, "but you will be soon. Sooner than you realize. Ah, Julia," he said, amused by her fit of temper, "we will have such marvelous children. They will have your fire and my intelligence."

Alek knew when her eyes drifted shut that she wasn't envisioning their offspring, but was desperately fighting to hold on to her temper. Once she accepted their marriage, she would make him a splendid lover. Already he'd sampled the passion and power that simmered within her. Soon, in her own time, she would come to him, willing and warm. He'd be waiting. He hadn't expected the fire to kindle this soon, but he was prepared to be her husband.

Convinced of her eventual submission, Alek saun-tered back into the living room, turned on the televi-sion and sat back to hear the nightly news.

No man had ever infuriated her more. Alek was a puzzle. It had demanded every ounce of courage she'd ever possessed to confront him with the truth. He'd been so blasé about it, as if he'd suspected her to de-fault on their agreement from the first. As if he'd been calmly waiting for her to defy him with the truth.

Then to have him casually announce it was too late to change her mind. It was too much. She'd rather rot in jail than make love to such an uncaring, ill-tempered, scheming . . .

Her mind stopped and suddenly she felt tired. If anyone had been scheming, it was her. Exhaustion per-meated her bones, and it was almost more than she could do to finish the dishes. Alek sat in her living room, watching television. Undisturbed. Confident. Sure of himself.

"I'm going to bed," she announced shakily, praying with everything in her that he wouldn't follow her.

Alek casually reached for the TV controller and turned off the television. He was on his feet, following her into the master bedroom, before she had time to protest.

"I'm very tired." Her eyes pleaded with him. If she couldn't reason with him, then perhaps she could evoke sympathy. Bottom-of-the-barrel compassion was all that was left in her bag of tricks.

"I'm tired, as well." He stood at the opposite side of her bed and unfastened the buttons of his shirt.

Julia felt like weeping. "You expect to sleep in here?"

"You are my wife."

"Please." Her voice cracked.

He didn't pause in his ministrations, tugging the shirt free from his waist and working the gold links from his cuffs.

"I can't sleep with you." Her words were low and barely audible.

He turned back the bed covers. "We are married, Julia, and we will share this room. You needn't worry that I will claim my husbandly rights. I'm confident that in time you'll to come to me. You will, you know, and when you do, I'll be waiting. I can be patient when the prize is of such high value."

The presumptuousness of the man continued to astound her. "I can't . . . sleep with you," she repeated.

"I am not a monster, Julia, but a man." He stopped and looked to her as if expecting her to argue further with him.

"I don't understand you," she cried, nearly hysterical by now. "I've cheated you, lied to you, why do you still want me . . . you should be glad to be rid of me."

"You are my wife."

It demanded all Julia's energy just to hold up her head. This man confused her and she hadn't the resources to continue.

He pulled back the sheets and puffed up the pillow on his side of the bed, making certain she understood he wouldn't be dissuaded.

"I can't think clearly," she said, pressing her hands to her cheeks. "I'll sleep in the guest bedroom."

His eyes revealed his disappointment. "You're sure?"

She nodded. "For now."

"As you wish, then."

Listlessly she moved around the foot of the bed. She'd bungled this matter of marriage from the beginning.

"Julia." His voice was softly accented and warmly masculine. Something in the way he said her name gave her pause.

"I'm so sorry," she said before he could speak. The tears, the emotion and her pain leaked into her voice.

"For what?"

She shrugged. For another failure. For dragging him into a loveless marriage with an unwilling, cold wife. For countless unconfessed sins.

"You've spent this day and many more just like it fighting yourself. You're weary of the battle, aren't you?"

Julia nodded. He was behind her, moving closer. She should leave now, walk away from him before he started to make sense, before he convinced her there was hope for her. Hope for them. She couldn't allow it to happen, because ultimately she would disappoint and hurt him.

"I am your husband," he whispered, as he turned her into his arms. "Let me carry your burdens. I'll lighten your load. I'm here to be your helpmate, your friend, your lover. Let me take care of you, Julia. Let me love you." As he spoke, his mouth was drawing closer and closer to hers, until their breaths had merged and mingled.

As hard as she tried, Julia was unable to dredge up a single protest when his mouth settled firmly over hers. He kissed her the way a woman dreams a man will kiss her, with a gentleness that touched some long-buried spark within her.

Just when she'd adjusted to his tenderness, he altered the kiss, making it hot and fierce. He buried his hands deep into her hair, using the tip of his tongue to tease her with wantonly delicious games, coaxing her until she moaned and sighed and wordlessly begged for more.

Her eager response excited him and his tongue probed her mouth, pushing brazenly inside, filling her. Heat, fiery and uncontrolled, spread its feverish fingers through her aching body.

Alek sighed and her name spilled unevenly from his lips. He pleaded with her, his voice filled with need and tenderness. With unbridled desire.

"Come, be my wife."

Julia's eyes fluttered open. It took her a second to comprehend what he'd said. When she did, she shot her gaze to him, unable to speak. Her heart was pounding like an African drum deep in the jungle, tapping out a dire warning. One she'd best heed.

"I . . . need time."

He continued to hold her gaze. "All right."

Tears filled her eyes and she bit into her lower lip. "You're getting the short end of the stick with me, Alek."

"Short end of the stick?"

She smiled softly. "It means, you're getting less than you deserve."

"Let me be the judge of that. In time you'll come to me of your own accord. In time you'll want me as much as I do you."

"There are many things you don't know about me," she said, her words so low he had to strain to hear her.

"Tell me."

She shook her head. "Just remember, I warned you."

He reluctantly released her, maintaining the contact as long as possible. His hands slid down the full length of her arms and, catching her fingers, he held on to the tips with his own.

"Good night, my wife," he whispered, and turned away. "I shall be lonely without you."

Julia left the room quickly, knowing if she stayed a moment longer, she would end up in the bed next to Alek, and only God knew what would happen then.

Julia found it amazingly easy to avoid Alek. Their work schedules were vastly different. She left for the office early, before he awoke. In the afternoons she visited her grandmother then ate a quiet meal by herself. Generally she was preparing for bed about the time Alek returned from the laboratory.

He was working long, hard hours before putting the latest research advancements into production. From the weekly reports he continued to send her, she knew that they were speeding ahead with the marketing and distribution of Phoenix Paints. The advertising blitz had yet to be decided, but that was coming. Everything looked promising.

But then, it had looked promising three years earlier, too. Yet within the course of a single week she'd lost her father, been betrayed by the man she loved, and nearly destroyed a business that had been in the family for three generations.

Julia had learned harsh but valuable lessons about promises. Probably the most pain-filled lessons of her life. She'd come away convinced she could trust only a cherished few. Equally important, she'd discovered never, never to cash in on potential. A check in the mail wasn't money in the bank.

Dear heavens, she mused as she left the office, she was growing sickeningly philosophical. Perhaps that was what marriage did to a woman.

Marriage.

Even the word sounded strange in her mind. She was married, for better or for worse, married. After her ti-rade on their wedding night, when she'd pleaded, threatened and tried to reason with Alek, she'd decided Alek was right. There was no backing out now. They were married for better or for worse.

Her actions were prompted by a certain amount of pride. Jerry had made certain the news of her nuptials to Alek had been carried by the local newspapers. The business community and acquaintances would have learned of her marriage. It would be a matter of acute embarrassment to seek an annulment so soon after the ceremony.

Mentally she added weakness and vanity to her growing list of character defects.

"Julia," Ruth accused weakly when she entered the hospital room, "what are you doing here?"

Julia grinned as she leaned forward and kissed her grandmother's pale cheek. "It's good to see you, too."

"Alek will never forgive me."

"Alek is hard at work," she assured Ruth.

"But you're newlyweds."

Julia's gaze skirted past her grandmother's. "He's been so busy lately. I'd rather spend time with you than hurry home to an empty apartment."

"I worry," Ruth said, her voice growing weaker.

"Worry?" Julia prompted. "There's no need. Both our schedules are hectic just now. Coming here is the best thing for me.... That way, when Alek arrives home, I'm calm and relaxed."

"Good. He's such a dear boy. You married well.... I so want you to be happy—it's what you deserve. Your season of pain is past now that you have Alek."

Julia wished to avoid the subject of her husband. "Would you like me to read to you?"

"Please, from the book of Psalms, if you would?"

"Of course." Julia reached for the well-worn Bible and sat in the chair next to her grandmother's hospital bed and read for several minutes. Long past the time Ruth was asleep. Long past the dinner hour. Long past the time for her to leave for home.

The night was hot and muggy, the air heavy with heat. Her air-conditioning system must not be working properly because it felt like the hottest night of the year. Even her skimpy, baby-doll pajamas seemed clammy and constricting.

Sleep seemed to wander just beyond her grasp no matter how hard she tried to capture it. The night was still and dark and she flopped from her side onto her back, then to her side once more, attempting to catch the touch of a cool breeze. But there was none.

Another hour passed and she gave up the effort. Silently slipping from her bed, she moved into her living room, standing in front of the long window. A few scattered lights flickered from Puget Sound. The last ferry crossing before dawn, she guessed, on its way to Winslow on Bainbridge Island.

The lights from Alki Point gleamed in the distance.

Julia wasn't certain how long she stood there, looking into the stillness of the night. Raising her arms high above her head, she stretched, standing on her tiptoes. The thin fabric of her pajama top rustled against the underside of her breasts. Her hair felt damp and heavy and she lifted the long tresses from the back of her head and shook it, sending a spray of hair in a circle around her face. A sigh slipped from her lips as she lifted the ends of her baby-doll top and flapped them, creating a draft against her full breasts.

The briefest of noises sounded from behind her and she whirled around to see a shadow unfold from the chair. Alek stood. He wore only the bottom half of his pajamas and his hard chest glistened in the muted light.

"Alek." His name rushed from between her teeth.

"I couldn't sleep, either," he told her.

"How . . . long have you been here?" she demanded.

"I wasn't spying on you, if that's what you're insinuating."

"I . . . you surprised me, is all."

"Come sit with me."

She shook her head and watched as his jaw tightened at her refusal.

"We're married," he reminded her. "You can't continue to ignore me the rest of your life. We made a bargain, which has yet to be fulfilled."

Why he chose to bring up the subject of their marriage, Julia was not to know. They'd lived peaceably for nearly two weeks, barely seeing each other, rarely talking. She'd almost convinced herself they could continue like this forever.

"I don't want to talk about our marriage."

She sensed his irritation turn to amusement. "No, I don't imagine you do," he said with a deflated sigh.

"I'm sorry... I didn't mean to snap at you. It's just that I wasn't expecting you to be here."

"I forgive you. Now sit and we can talk."

Julia hesitated, then decided it would do more harm than good to refuse him. She chose a seat across from him and sank onto the sofa. Holding a decorative pillow to her stomach helped ease her discomfort over her state of undress, although not by much.

"How is your grandmother?"

"About the same. I talked to her doctor this afternoon and he said..." She paused and bit into her lower lip. "He said that we shouldn't expect her to return home again."

"Is she in much pain?"

"Yes, sometimes, although she tries to hide it from me. Listen, do you mind if we don't talk about Ruth, either?"

"Of course. I didn't mean to bring up a subject that causes you pain."

Julia lowered her gaze. "It's just that...she's so very important to me. Ruth's all the family Jerry and I have left."

"Your mother?"

"She died when I was fifteen, and my father," she added before Alek could ask, "three years ago... shortly after the fire."

Silence stretched between them. Julia's pressure on the pillow increased. Even in the darkened room, she could feel his smoldering gaze move caressingly over her. He wanted her and was growing impatient. Her heart pounded with dread and regret.

"Please don't look at me like that," she pleaded. It seemed as if his eyes were about to devour her. He wanted her to know how much he longed to make love to her. The memory of his kisses returned to haunt her and she shook her head, needing to dispel the image before it took root in her mind, took root in her heart, and left her yearning for more.

"You're very beautiful."

She'd heard those meaningless words before. Beauty was fleeting and counted for little of real value in life. Being outwardly attractive hadn't made her a better judge of character. It didn't do one iota of good as far as her grandmother's health was concerned. If anything, it had been a curse, because it attracted an unsavory element to her.

"This makes you sad?"

She shrugged. "Beauty means nothing."

"You are wise to recognize as much."

"Then why do you find it necessary to mention it?"

"Because you were not beautiful when we first met. It's only been recently that I've come to appreciate that you are a real woman."

A real woman. Julia nearly laughed aloud.

"This is what makes being married to you and not sleeping with you so difficult. Have you reconsidered yet, my love? Come with me, share my bed."

"I . . . can't, please don't ask it of me." Her response was immediate. Tossing the pillow aside, she zoomed to her feet, needing to escape. "Good night, Alek."

He didn't answer her and she didn't look back as she rushed to her room. Her heart was roaring like thunder in her ears by the time she reached the bed. Once again she felt like the fox in an English hunt, and the sound of the dogs was closing in on her.

"Julia."

She nearly leaped off the mattress when she looked up and found Alek framed in her doorway. Her breath froze in her lungs as alarm raced through her blood.

"Someday you won't run from me like a frightened rabbit."

"I wasn't running from you." It was a bold-faced lie and they both knew it, yet Julia persisted in claiming otherwise.

His smile was uneven and a scant cocky. "Someday you will voluntarily come to me."

She wasn't going to argue with him. He watched her closely in the muted moonlight and she studied him. With a start she realized her top had inched up over her abdomen and exposed her breasts. Furiously she tugged it down and glared at him as though he'd purposely arranged the immodest display.

"As I said earlier, you are very beautiful."

He smiled roguishly at her. "I'm growing impatient, Julia. There's no telling how much longer my good nature will hold."

After a sleepless, frustrating night, Julia was in no mood to deal with a long list of complicated problems. Virginia, her middle-aged secretary, looked apologetic when Julia arrived at the office early the following morning.

"Get my brother on the line when you can," Julia instructed. Her mind was made up, she wanted out of this farce of a marriage.

"He's already called for you." Her secretary hugged a file folder against her chest. "He asked that you call him the moment you arrive."

Julia reached for her phone and punched out the extension number. Jerry answered on the first ring. "Come down to my office," he instructed impatiently.

"Now?"

"Right now."

"What's wrong?" she demanded.

"You'll find out soon enough."

This morning was quickly going from bad to worse, sort of the same way her life had been headed. From the frying pan directly into the fire. She paused, catching herself. Her thoughts hadn't always been so negative. When had this started? The wedding? No, she decided, long before then. Three years earlier, but she wondered why she was aware of it now.

The answer to that was lost on her as she rounded the corner that led to the suite of offices her brother occupied on the floor below her own.

"Jerry, what's this all about?" she asked before she noticed Alek. She halted when she saw her husband sitting in the chair waiting for her.

"Sit down," her brother instructed, motioning toward Alek.

Julia did as he asked. Jerry paced back and forth behind his desk. "I was contacted this morning by the INS people. Damn, I knew this would happen, I just didn't expect it would be quite so soon."

"We're being investigated?" Alek asked.

Jerry nodded. "The two of you are going to have to convince them you're madly in love. Do you think you can do it?"

Julia noticed he focused his gaze on her. "Ah..."

"Yes," Alek responded without hesitation.

"Julia, what about you?"

"Ah..." She'd never been good with pretense.

"She'll convince them." Alek revealed far more confidence in her than she had in herself. "It won't take much work." He reached for her hand, gripping it in his own. "All we'll need is a little practice, isn't that right, my love?"

Chapter Five

Only seconds earlier Julia had decided she wanted out of this charade of a marriage, no matter what the price. Just when it seemed that very thing was about to happen, she discovered herself willing to do whatever was necessary to keep their relationship intact.

Counseling. That was what she needed, Julia decided. Intensive counseling. She wasn't an indecisive woman; that would be a death knell for someone in her position. Generally she knew what she wanted and went after it with a determination that left everyone in her wake shaking their heads in wonder.

It was Aleksandr who managed to ruffle her so. It was Alek who left her feeling as though she were walking along the banks of a pond filled with bubbling quicksand.

"Julia?" Jerry turned the full force of his attention on her. "Can you do it?"

Both men were studying her. Could she pretend to be in love with Alek? Pretend her very happiness hinged on spending the rest of her life with him? Could she?

"I . . . I don't know."

"Shall I repeat what's at stake here?" Jerry offered.

It wasn't necessary; he'd gone over the consequences of their actions when he'd proposed the idea of her marrying Alek. The government did much more than frown upon such unions. There was the possibility of jail time if they weren't able to convince the INS of their sincerity.

"Julia knows," Alek assured Jerry calmly. "Isn't that right, my love?"

She lowered her eyes. "I'm fully aware of what could happen."

"That's fine and dandy, but can you be convincing enough to persuade the immigration people?" Jerry demanded.

She nodded slowly, thoughtfully. It wasn't a question of being able to pull this off with the finesse required, but it would mean lowering the guard on her heart. The most important factor wasn't her ability to fool the INS, but resurrecting the protective shield protecting her against the emotional pull she felt toward Alek. Already she was attracted to him, both physically and emotionally. Otherwise she wouldn't have participated in or enjoyed the few times they'd kissed. Otherwise she'd never have agreed to marry him.

To complicate matters, the attachment was growing stronger each day. She found herself thinking about him at the oddest times. As hard as it was to admit, Julia discovered she enjoyed his company and looked forward to the brief time they spent together each day.

"You're sure?" Jerry asked, sounding anything but.

"Positive," she said, chancing a look in Alek's direction. He caught her eye and smiled reassuringly. His hand reached for hers and he squeezed her fingers.

"We'll do just fine," Alek said to Jerry. "Just you wait and see. What both of you fail to realize is that Julia and I did marry for love."

"Stop pacing," Alek said, more testily than he intended. The INS officer was due in fifteen minutes and Julia was understandably nervous. Unable to sit still, she stalked the living room like a caged cougar.

"Walking helps take my mind off the interview," Julia snapped back.

The tension between them was thick enough to slice and serve for dinner. That would hurt their case more than anything they said or did. The man or woman doing the interview might sense the strain immediately and count it against them.

"You should know more about me," Julia said, whirling around to face him as if this was a new thought. "The kind of toothpaste I use and stuff like that."

"Don't be ridiculous."

"I'm not.... That's exactly the kind of questions he'll ask."

"Julia, my love," he said patiently, "a man doesn't pay attention to such things. Not unless there's a reason. Now relax."

"How can you be so calm?" she snapped, slapping her hands against her sides. "Our future hinges on the outcome of this meeting. There's a very real possibility of my doing jail time for involving myself in this... marriage." Her arms, which had bounced in several different directions, seemed to have lost their purpose and fell lifelessly to her sides. "I'm not the only one who has a good deal at stake with this. The future of your mother and sister hinge on the outcome, as well. Didn't you mention you've already seen to the necessary paperwork for them?"

"I'm aware of the consequences."

"Then how can you be so blasted calm?"

"Very simple, my love." He said this evenly and without emotion as he leaned forward, gripped her around the waist and brought her down into his lap.

Julia struggled at first. "Stop," she said, wiggling against him. "What the hell are you trying to do?"

He let her struggle, but her efforts were weak at best. His arms were around her and he sensed her yielding. Taking advantage of her acquiescence, he brushed his face against her hair. She'd left it down, at his request, and he gathered the length in his hands, loving the clean jasmine scent of it.

"Alek, are you mad?"

"In a moment, love," he promised as he moistened a trail of kisses along her throat and shoulder. "That's better," he whispered as he felt her tight muscles loosen. "Much better."

"I... I don't think we should be doing this."

"What?" he quizzed as his hand caressed her back in a slow, soothing motion. "This?" He eased her back against the chair until her hair spilled over the back of his arm. A whisper of a sigh escaped her as he pressed his lips to hers. A surge of hot desire rode through him as her trembling lips welcomed him, parting for the exploration of his tongue.

Julia felt hot, cold and shaky in his arms, but no more so than he. They'd kissed a handful of times and each incidence had been a battle for him. He'd always come out the victor. His wife had balked at his touch in the beginning, then gradually she opened herself to him until he was so damn needy he ached for hours afterward.

She must possess some inner sonar that was able to detect at which point her pulling away would cause him the most agony. He was left feeling he'd won the battle and lost the war.

This time the skirmish between them was over even before it started. Julia accepted his kiss with little more than a token protest. Perhaps she was ready for more. God help him, Alek was, and had been from the first.

His heart was pounding as he slipped his hand beneath her pale pink sweater and caressed the smooth, satiny skin of her abdomen. She accepted his touch and encouraged him; he leisurely progressed upward to the full swell of her breasts. He continued kissing her, slanting his mouth over hers, the action fierce and demanding.

He broke off the kiss and spoke, telling her how badly he needed to taste her. He pleaded with her as only a man who needs his wife can implore. It wasn't until he read the confusion in her eyes that he realized he'd spoken in his native tongue. His English was hopeless, just then. Without waiting for her permission, he reached behind her and unfastened the snaps to her bra. She didn't stop him, nor did she assist him. His hand caught her breast as it sprang free and overfilled his palm. His thumb circled her nipple and he was delighted with the eager way her body responded to his manipulations.

"Alek..."

"Shh." He silenced her with a lengthy, breath-robbing kiss that left him trembling. His torture had only begun, he realized. If it was possible that a man could die with wanting, then Alek was ready to send for a priest to issue him the last rites.

His mouth was moist and hot as it closed over her breast. He suckled her and he wasn't sure whose sigh of pleasure echoed in his ear, his own or Julia's. Bunching her breasts together, he divided his attention between both, creating a slick, moist trail from the tip of one breast to the other. She arched and bucked, creating a new brand of agony for him as she inadvertently stroked the strength of his erection.

Julia's fingers were digging into his shoulders. He felt the rapid beat of her heart and heard the ragged echo of her breath as it rasped in his ear.

The doorbell chimed and Alek would have opted to ignore it if Julia hadn't frozen and then leaped from his lap as though she were on fire.

"Oh, my goodness," she cried. Her face was a rich shade of red as she swept the hair from her face. "The INS interviewer is here." Her eyes round globes, she stared at him as if he had the magical power to make everything right.

"That would be my guess."

"Alek." Her voice wobbled as she quickly readjusted her clothes. "I'm scared."

"Don't be. Everything will be fine," he promised. He gave her a moment to fuss with her hair before he stood, kissed her lightly on the lips and answered the door.

Although Alek appeared outwardly composed, he was as shaken as Julia. And not because their future hung in the balance with this interview. His head reeled with the aftershocks of their lovemaking. He hadn't meant for matters to progress quite so far, so fast. A few kisses, he thought, to take the edge off their nervousness. Within another few moments he would have carried her to his bed and they would have been so deeply involved with each other he wouldn't have allowed anything to interrupt them.

"Hello," Alek greeted, opening the door to admit a lanky, official-looking gentleman. He wore a crisp business suit and from the tight set of his mouth, Alek guessed he would brook no foolishness. His features were sharp and unfriendly.

"Patrick O'Dell," he said.

"My name is Alek and this is my wife, Julia," Alek said.

Julia stood on the far side of the room and her smile was fleeting and strained. "Welcome to our home, Mr. O'Dell. Would you care to sit down?"

"Thank you." He moved into the living room and didn't pause to look at the view. Indeed there might not have been one for all the notice O'Dell took. He sat on the recliner they'd recently vacated and set his briefcase on the coffee table.

Alek moved to Julia's side and gripped her hand in his. Together they ventured to the sofa opposite him and sat down.

Mr. O'Dell removed a file from his briefcase. His gaze scanned the contents and he frowned with clear disapproval. "How did you two meet?"

"Through my brother," Julia responded quickly. "He'd met Alek several years earlier while on a tour of Europe. The two corresponded for a number of years and then after the fire..." She hesitated and looked to Alek.

"Jerry offered me a job in this country three years ago. I've lived here for the past two."

"Tell me about your work."

Alek answered the questions thoroughly, minimizing his importance to Conrad Industries. There was no need to raise suspicions.

"Alek is a gifted biochemist," Julia added with unnecessary enthusiasm. "The company was nearly ruined a few years back following a large fire. I don't know what would have become of Conrad Industries if it hadn't been for Alek."

Although he smiled, Alek was groaning inwardly. Julia was offering far more information than necessary. He wished now that he'd gone over with her what they planned to say. Jerry had advised them to do so, but Alek had felt their spontaneity would serve them better than a series of practiced responses.

"In other words, you needed Mr. Berinski."

"Yes, very much so." Julia was nothing if not honest.

"Do you continue to need him?" The interviewer pressed.

"No," Alek answered before Julia could.

"I disagree," she returned, looking briefly to Alek. "I find we need him now more than ever. The new line of paints Alek has been working on for the past two years is ready to be marketed. That's only the beginning of the ideas he's developing.''

Alek's concern mounted as O'Dell made a notation.

"My husband has worked hard on this project. He deserves to reap the fruits of his labors." To her credit, Julia didn't stumble over the word "husband." She'd said it a number of times since their marriage and it always seemed to cause her some difficulty.

"You give me more credit than my due, my dear," he said, feeling as though they'd dug themselves into a pit.

"Nonsense," Julia continued, warming to her subject. "Alek is a genius."

Another notation.

Alek squeezed Julia's fingers, willing her to stop speaking, but the more he tried to discourage her, the more she felt it was necessary to continue.

"If you two held each other in such high esteem, why did you wait until the last moment before Alek's visa expired before you agreed to marry?"

"Love isn't always planned," Julia answered quickly. "No one completely understands matters of the heart, do they? I know I didn't." She glanced shyly toward Alek.

"I understand why the INS is suspicious of our union," Alek added. "We realized you would be when we decided to go ahead and marry. It made no difference."

Another notation, this one made with sharp jagged movements of the pen.

There were several more questions, which they answered as completely and forthrightly as possible. Alek was uncertain of how well they were coming across.

He'd rarely seen Julia more animated and, to his surprise, sincere. When he first learned of the interview, his one concern had been Julia, but she'd proved to be his strongest asset.

If he was forced to return to Prushkin, Alek would go, because he had no other choice. He hadn't dwelled on the consequences, refusing to allow any negative suggestions to enter his mind. He realized as they were speaking how very much he would hate leaving Julia.

"I think that answers everything," O'Dell said, closing his file and placing it back inside his briefcase.

The unexpectedness of his announcement caught Alek off guard.

"That's all?" Apparently Julia was as surprised as he was. "You don't want to know what brand of toothpaste Alek uses or about his personal habits?"

The INS official smiled for the first time. "We leave that sort of interrogation for the movies. It's obvious to me you two deeply care for each other. I wish all my assignments were as easy to determine."

"Will I need to sign anything?" Julia asked.

"No," O'Dell said as he stood. "I'll file my report by the end of the week. I don't believe there's any reason for us to be in contact with you, at least not now. I appreciate your agreeing to see me on such short notice."

Alek stood in order to escort Mr. O'Dell to the door. Julia seemed to be in a state of shock. She sat on the thick cushion, her mouth dangling open, staring up at the INS official with a baffled, uncertain look.

"Thank you again for your trouble," Patrick O'Dell said when Alek opened the front door.

"Julia and I should be the ones thanking you."

The two men exchanged brief handshakes. Alek closed the door with such relief that he leaned against the frame. He expelled his breath in a long, slow exercise, unaware he'd been holding it.

"Julia." He whispered her name as he returned to the living room. She hadn't moved. "We did it."

She nodded as though she was in a trance.

"You were fantastic."

Her eyes went to him and she blinked as if she didn't recognize who he was. "Me?"

"You were forthright and honest. At first I was worried, convinced you were giving him far more information than was necessary. Then I realized that was what convinced him. You acted as though you had nothing to hide. As if our staying married meant all the world to you. It wasn't anything I said or did, it was you."

"Me?" she repeated again, sounding close to breaking into tears.

She looked as if she'd topple at any moment. Alek knelt down in front of her and gripped her hands in his. "Are you all right?"

Sniffling, she shook her head. The ordeal had been a strain, but he was surprised by her response. Julia wasn't the type of woman to buckle easily. Nor did she weep without provocation. Something was definitely going on inside that sweet head of hers.

"What's wrong?" he asked tenderly, resisting the urge to take her into his arms and kiss her senseless.

Tears filled her eyes and she made a valiant effort to blink them away. "I think I'll go lie down for a while. I'm sure I'll be fine in a few minutes."

Alek didn't want her to leave. He was hoping they could pick up where they'd left off before they'd been interrupted by O'Dell's arrival. The craving she'd created in him had yet to be satisfied. He wanted her to share his bed. She was his wife, and it was where she belonged.

Alek had learned enough about Julia to recognize she'd come to him in her own sweet time, when she was ready and not before. God help him, he prayed he had the patience to wait her out.

As she lay in her bed, pretending to nap, Julia realized it wasn't until the INS official had stood to leave that she recognized how sincere she was in what she'd said to the man. She'd answered the questions as candidly as possible, warming to the subject the longer she spoke. As she continued, it struck her that Alek was as important to her personally as he was the company. Perhaps more so. The realization came as an unexpected shock.

He'd been gentle and patient and kind. His kisses stirred her very soul. That sounded fanciful, she realized, and a little overdramatic, but she was at a loss to explain it otherwise.

Heaven help her, she was falling in love with him. It wasn't supposed to happen this way. She didn't want to love him, didn't want to care about him. After Phoenix Paints were released and he'd established his mother and sister in the country, she wanted Alek out of her life. It was what she'd planned, what she was expecting to happen. Involving her heart would be both foolish and dangerous. She'd already learned her lesson when it came to trusting a man. Roger had taught her well.

"Julia?" His voice came on the soft wings of a whisper, followed by several Russian words. She kept her eyes closed, not wanting Alek to know she was awake from her nap. Every now and again, Alek reverted to his mother tongue, but generally it was only when they were kissing.

Kissing. Her face filled with color at the memory of their exchange. She couldn't believe the liberties Alek had taken with her earlier that afternoon. Liberties she'd encouraged and enjoyed. She would be forever grateful that Mr. O'Dell had chosen just then to arrive.

Because of her nap that afternoon, Julia was restlessness and unable to sleep that evening. Looking to sidestep any questions from Alek, she'd gone to the hospital to visit Ruth later that same afternoon.

The condo was empty when she returned and Julia guessed Alek had gone to the laboratory to work. Feeling somewhat guilty, she microwaved her dinner, hoping her husband would pick up something to eat for himself while he was out.

He wasn't back by the time she showered and readied for bed. She should have been grateful, instead she found herself waiting and watching for him. It was nearly eleven when she heard the front door open. Light from the kitchen spilled into the hallway outside her bedroom as he rummaged around, apparently looking for dinner.

Battling with a second bout of guilt didn't improve her disposition any. Knowing next to nothing about cooking should prove beyond a suggestion of a doubt that she made him a terrible wife. Another, more domesticated woman would have been knitting by the fireplace, awaiting his return with a five-course meal warming in the oven. Forget that it was summer, this imaginary dutiful wife would have a cozy fire roaring away.

After she'd seen to her husband's physical appetite, she'd satisfy the carnal by removing her housecoat and standing before him dressed in a sheer nightie.

But Alek hadn't married the ideal wife; instead he was stuck with her.

"Julia?"

She was so surprised by the sound of her name that she lifted her head from the pillow.

"I hope I didn't wake you."

"No... I hadn't gone to sleep yet." She sat up in bed and tugged the sheets protectively around her.

His shadow loomed against the opposite wall like an irate monster. Try as she would, Julia couldn't make him into one.

"How's your grandmother?"

She shrugged. It became more apparent with every visit that Ruth wouldn't last much longer. A part of Julia clung to her grandmother and another part struggled to willingly release Ruth from this life and the pain that accompanied it.

"You were at the laboratory?"

Alek nodded.

"Is it really necessary for you to work so many hours?"

Alek crossed his arms and leaned against the door-jamb. His eyes seemed dark and limpid. "Work helps me deal with my frustration."

He didn't need to clarify his answer. Julia knew he was referring to the sexual disappointment of their marriage.

When she didn't respond, he sighed and added, "I figured out why everything went so smoothly with the INS official. You, my dear, sweet wife, are in love with me."

The audacity of the comment was too much to overlook. "I'm what?"

"In love with me," he repeated with supreme confidence. "I was a fool not to recognize it earlier."

"You're badly in need of reality therapy," Julia said, making her words as scathing as she could. "That's the most ridiculous thing you've ever said,"

"Wait, I promise you it'll get better. Much better." How cocky he sounded, so sure of himself that it was all she could do not to fall prey to his teasing.

"Much worse, you mean," she said with an exaggerated yawn. "Now if you don't mind, I'd like to get some sleep."

"Later. We need to talk."

"Alek, please, it's nearly midnight."

"You've already admitted you hadn't been to sleep."

"Exactly," she argued. "I need my rest."

"So do I." His words were heavy with meaning.

"Leave it until the morning," she suggested next.

"You agreed to be my wife. How long is it going to take before you live up to your end of our bargain? How long, my love?"

"I...already explained I need time...to adjust to everything. Why are you doing this?" she cried, furious with him for dragging out a subject she considered closed. "I refuse to be pressured into making love just because you've got an overactive libido."

"Pressured," he echoed, and a deep frown formed. He rubbed his hand over his face and sighed audibly. "I've been waiting for you since our wedding night. As I told you before, I'm a patient man, but even my good nature has limits."

"We've only been married a few weeks," she protested.

"Ah, but you love me. You all but proved it this afternoon. There's no need to wait any longer, Julia. I need you, and you need me." With a knowing smile, he turned and walked away.

The comment irritated her so much she couldn't bear to let it go unanswered. Gripping her pillow with both hands, she threw it after him. It slammed against the doorframe with a soft plunk that was barely discernible. Alek heard it, however, because he turned around and started laughing.

The following morning, as was her habit, Julia rose early and stood barefoot in the kitchen while she waited for the first cup of coffee to filter into the glass pot. The aroma of Colombian beans filled the kitchen.

"'Morning." Alek spoke groggily from behind her.

Julia's eyes flew open. Normally Alek didn't rise until after she'd left for work. "'Morning," she greeted with little enthusiasm.

"Did you sleep well?"

No. "Fine. How about you?" Her attention remained focused on the coffeepot. She didn't dare turn around and confront her rumpled, groggy husband. Knowing he was only a few feet behind her activated her imagination. His hair was probably unkempt and his eyes drowsy and soft, the way hers were. He'd look sexy and appealing.

"Julia," he whispered, moving forward. He slipped his arms around her waist and nuzzled her neck. "We can't go on like this. We're married, when are you going to recognize as much?"

She braced her hands against his, which were joined at her abdomen. His lips located the pulse pounding at the side of her neck and he rubbed his mouth there, moistening the sensitized area with his tongue.

Julia's breath caught in her throat. "Alek, please, don't."

"Stop?" He raised his head as though he couldn't believe she meant it.

"Yes." His hand eased upward and cupped her breast. His hand was as gentle as it was unexpected. Her nipple hardened at the contact and throbbed with the ministrations of his thumb.

"I couldn't sleep for want of you," he whispered.

Her throat felt as dry as the Nevada desert. Speaking was impossible. His other hand joined the first, finding her other breast.

"All I could think about was how good you tasted and how much I wanted to hold you and love you again."

The coffee had finished brewing, but for the life of her, Julia couldn't make herself move.

"I know you want me. Why do you torture us so?"

"I...have to get to work." Each syllable was a triumph.

"Let me make love to you," Alek urged, his mouth close to her ear. "Just once, that's all I'm asking."

"Once? That will fulfill our bargain?"

Her breasts seemed to swell and throb with the caressing motions of his hands. He didn't answer her with words, instead he turned her around so they stood eye to eye, face-to-face. Heart to heart.

She moistened her mouth, anticipating his kiss. Alek didn't disappoint her. He kissed her with a hunger that staggered and intimidated her. His tongue touched hers and his arms came around her, pulling her against him. His hands stroked her back as he continued kissing her, not allowing her to protest, had she tried. Before she was conscious of what he was doing, he'd eased his way past the elastic waistband of her pajama bottoms. He tucked his hands beneath her derriere and lifted her slightly upward until she was flush against him. He was hard with need, his desire like a steel wedge between them.

"Oh, Alek," Julia whispered, dragging her mouth from his. Her breasts were heaving as she struggled to move away from him. Alek released her with obvious reluctance. "I . . . I'll be late for the office." She didn't wait for him to argue with her, but rushed instead toward her bedroom. Toward sanity.

By the time Julia reached her office, she was in a rare mood. She blamed Alek for this. As much as she wished it were true, she wasn't made of stone. She was flesh and blood and heaven help her, a woman. He couldn't kiss and touch her without her experiencing a certain sexual yearning.

It meant nothing. He insisted she was in love with him, but Julia knew it was talk. All of it was bull, in order to persuade her to allow him to make love to her.

Sweet talk, with a single purpose in mind. To seduce her.

Julia had been seduced before, by an artful master. In comparison, Alek was so much more honest in his aim and, therefore, easier to defend against. She refused to give in to his pressure, subtle or otherwise. As for misleading him, she had, but only in a limited capacity.

Furious now, she marched into her office, reached for her phone and dialed Jerry's extension. "Can you come up?" she barked.

"Yes. Is everything all right?"

"No."

Jerry paused. "I thought everything went hunky-dory with the inspector."

"It did, as far as I know. This has to do with Alek."

"I'll be right up," her brother assured her.

She was pacing her office with military precision steps when he arrived. Julia paused, angry with herself, feeling close to tears and not understanding why.

"What's wrong?" he asked, his concern evident in his eyes.

"I ... there's a problem."

"With what?"

"Whom," she corrected. "Aleksandr Berinski."

Jerry frowned, then sighed with resignation. "What's he done?"

"Everything ... Listen, I don't want to get into this. Let me make this as plain and as simple as I can. I think it's time he moved. One of us has to and it's either him or me."

Chapter Six

"You want Alek out of your condo?" Jerry repeated.

"You heard me right the first time." She flared impatiently. "Our marriage has been sanctioned by the INS. What reason do we have to continue with this charade?"

"Julia..."

She'd heard that tone of voice all too often. "Jerry, I'm not in any mood to argue with you." She walked around her desk and claimed her seat. Reaching for a file from her in-basket, she opened it and focused her attention there. "I'll leave the arrangements in your hands."

"Do you plan to talk this over with Alek?"

She hadn't thought of that. "It...won't be necessary. He'll get the picture once he hears from you."

"I won't do it."

Her brother's refusal caught her attention as nothing else could have. "What do you mean, you won't do it?"

"First, I won't have you treating Alek as though he were a pest you're looking to discard."

"It wouldn't be like that," she argued, realizing even as she spoke that Jerry was right. She couldn't treat Alek this way simply because she feared he was right and she was falling in love with him.

"Secondly," her brother continued, "it'd be crazy to throw everything away now. You believe that just because you've passed some interview with an INS inspector, you're in the clear. Think again, Julia. That's exactly the kind of thing the INS is expecting to happen."

"They won't know."

"Don't count on it. They make it their business to find out this sort of thing."

"Jerry, please." She rarely pleaded with her brother. "The man's impossible.... I've done my duty. What more to you expect of me?"

"Alek is your husband."

"You're beginning to sound just like him. He frightens me.... He makes me feel things I don't want to feel. I'm afraid, Jerry, really afraid." She was close to tears and covered her mouth, fearing she'd break down.

"I don't know what to do," Jerry said with a sympathetic shrug. "I wish I did, for your sake. Alek's, too."

The frustration came at her in waves. Tidal waves. One after the other, each gaining in intensity.

Her mood didn't improve when two hours later Alek unexpectedly showed up. He walked into her office without waiting for her secretary to announce him. Julia happened to be on the phone at the time and she glanced up, irritated by the intrusion. Alek glared at her as if it demanded the full strength of his will not to rip the phone out of her hands. Every minute she delayed appeared to infuriate him further.

He took to pacing and paused every other step to turn and scowl in her direction.

Julia finished the conversation as quickly as she could without being rude, and without letting him believe he was intimidating her.

"You wanted something?" she asked calmly as she replaced the telephone receiver.

Anger was etched plainly on his features. "You bet I do. I understand you spoke to Jerry this morning about one of us moving. I want to know what the hell is going on in that thick skull of yours."

Julia folded her hands atop her desk. "It seemed the logical thing to do."

"Why?"

She stood, feeling at a distinct disadvantage sitting. He loomed over her as if he were some feudal lord, intent on issuing justice. "It makes sense. The only reason we were living together was for show because..."

"We're living together, my dear wife, because we're married."

"In name only."

He muttered something blistering in his mother tongue and for once Julia was grateful she couldn't understand him.

"You deny your vows. You deny me my rights as your husband. Then you abuse my pride by involving your brother. You ask for patience and then stab me in the back."

"I...explained on our wedding day I need time. I let you know you were being cheated in this marriage. You can't say I didn't warn you." Contacting Jerry had been wrong. She was frightened and growing more so each day. No longer could she ignore the powerful attraction she felt for Alek. No longer could she ignore his touch. He was chipping away at the solid foundation of her protection from feelings. From love. He was worming his way into her life and into her heart. She had to do something.

"You are my wife," Alek shouted.

Julia closed her eyes and jumped at the fierce anger in his voice.

"I'm not a very good one," she whispered.

"We are married, Julia, and the sooner you accept the fact, the better." He turned away from her and stalked to the door.

"I . . . don't know that I can."

At her words, he spun around.

They stood no more than a few feet apart, yet an entire ocean might have lain between them. He was furious with her and she with him.

"I may never be your wife, the way you want." Julia didn't know what drove her to taunting him. Her words were akin to waving a red flag in front of a snorting bull. And she knew it. Yet her fear compelled her to do and say things she never would have ordinarily.

Alek accepted the challenge with a low laugh. "We'll see about that, my lovely wife."

He marched toward her with the determination of Eisenhower advancing on the beaches of Normandy. With a small cry of alarm, Julia hurried behind her desk, putting as much distance between them as possible.

Alek countered every move Julia made. He wasn't going to allow her to escape without retribution and she knew it. At the same moment, she realized she wanted him. Needed him. And that frightened her half to death.

"I'll scream for help," she threatened, leaping to the right.

"Go ahead." Alek didn't appear the least bit concerned, which infuriated her even more.

"You need me," he shouted. "When are you going to admit it? When?"

"I don't need any man."

Venting his frustration seemed to be helping Alek, as well. She took two steps in one direction, his movements rebutted hers. She went three. He went four.

They'd circled the desk by then and were going around it a second time when Alek spoke.

"You're afraid, aren't you? Afraid you aren't woman enough to hold me. Afraid you aren't woman enough to satisfy me. That's what's behind all this, isn't it? Don't you realize, my love, how wrong you are? We need each other. Why do you insist on playing this senseless game?"

Stricken, Julia froze. It felt as if he'd stabbed her with the truth, as if she were dying in the face of honesty. Alek had identified her nameless fears, hurled them at her and left them for her to answer.

"Julia?"

She sobbed once, the sound nearly hysterical as she backed away from him. The game was over. The fun, if it had ever been fun, had ended.

"I didn't mean . . ."

She stopped him by holding out her arm.

He cursed under his breath, and reaching for her, hauled her into his arms. Without pause he lowered his head and covered her mouth, sealing their lips together in a wild kiss. The craziness increased with each impatient twist of their heads, which jerked one direction and then another as if they were intent on devouring each other. He nipped her lips, bullied her with his tongue and claimed her mouth again and again with a growing frenzied desperation.

Her breasts tingled and her body grew hot as she rotated her hips against him. His powerful hands trapped her, imprisoning her. Thigh met thigh and there was no ignoring his aroused state, which settled against her lower stomach.

His hands were busy with the zipper at the back of her straight, no-nonsense business skirt. The sound of it lowering rang like a buzz saw in Julia's ears. She made a token protest, which he cut off with a bone-melting kiss.

"I'm through fighting you," he whispered. "You're mine and always will be."

She wanted to argue with him, wanted to push him away, but he claimed her mouth, gently fitting his lips to hers. They were so close Julia felt as if they were drawing in the same breath, as if they required only one heart to beat between them.

Sobbing, she looped her arms around his neck and buried her face in his neck, drawing in deep, uneven breaths. Not understanding her desperate need, she clung to him as a low cry threaded through her lips. The grief she experienced was overwhelming. She was lamenting the wasted, sorry years she'd closed herself off from life. Ever since her father's death and Roger's betrayal, she'd lived in limbo, rejecting love and laughter. Rejecting and punishing herself.

"Julia," Alek whispered, stroking her head, "what is it?"

She shook her head, refusing to answer.

"Say it," he demanded softly, sitting in her chair and taking her with him so she was nestled in his lap. "Tell me you need me. Tell me you want me, too."

She sobbed and with tears streaming down her face, she nodded.

"That's not good enough. I want the words."

"I... need you, Alek. Oh God, I'm so scared."

He held her, kissed her gently, reassured her while she pressed her head to his shoulder and cried until her tears were spent.

"There'll be no more talk of either of us moving out of our home, understand?"

She nodded. "I don't know why you put up with me."

"You don't?" he asked, chuckling softly. "I have the feeling you'll figure it out soon enough, my love."

Her intercom hummed and her secretary's voice echoed through the silence. "Your nine-thirty appointment is here."

Her gaze regretfully met Alek's.

"Send whoever it is away," Alek urged.

"I... I can't do that."

"I know," he said, and kissed the tip of her nose. He released her slowly.

Just when Julia was convinced her day couldn't possibly get any worse, she received a call from Virginia Mason Hospital. Her grandmother had slipped into a coma.

Jerry was away at the time, so she left a message for her brother, canceled her appointments for the rest of the day and drove directly to the hospital.

Julia recognized the instant she walked into her grandmother's room that Ruth's hold on life was little more than a slender thread. Her aged heart was failing. Odd, but Julia suddenly felt as though her own heart was in jeopardy.

In the past several years she'd faced a handful of crises. It had started with the fire that had nearly destroyed the business and their family. Her father's death had followed. Immediately afterward she'd realized Roger had used her, had sold out her family. And her.

Ruth, her beloved Ruth, was dying, and Julia was powerless to stop it. She was terribly afraid. For the past several months she'd stood by helplessly and watched her grandmother's health degenerate.

Sitting at Ruth's bedside, Julia could almost hear the older woman's calming voice. "My death is inevitable," the unspoken words rang in her heart, "but not unwelcome."

Silently Julia pleaded with her grandmother to hold on just a little while longer, to give her time to adjust, to grant her a few days to gather her courage around her. Even as she spoke, Julia recognized how selfish she was being, thinking of herself, of her own pain. But she couldn't make herself stop praying that God would spare her grandmother.

"You have walked through your pain," the still, silent voice in Julia's heart continued. "The journey has made you wiser and far stronger than you realize."

Julia wanted to argue. She didn't feel strong. Not then, not when it seemed Ruth was about to be taken from her. She felt pushed to the limits, looking both ways toward despair and hope, doubt and faith. Not knowing which way to turn.

An hour passed as Julia struggled against her grief, refusing to allow it to overwhelm her. Fear controlled her, she recognized. The knowledge that if she ever let herself go she might never regain her sanity never left her.

"Please," she pleaded aloud, praying Ruth heard her. It was a selfish prayer, of a frightened child.

Jerry arrived, looking pale and shaken himself.

"What happened?"

Julia shrugged. Their grandmother's physician, Dr. Silverman, had been in earlier to explain the medical reasons. Most of what he'd said had meant only one thing. Ruth was close to death.

"She's in a coma," Julia answered. "I talked to her doctor earlier. He's surprised she's hung on this long."

Her brother pulled out a chair and sat down next to Julia. "I love this old woman, really love her."

"What are we going to do without her, Jerry?"

Her brother didn't seem to have any suggestions. "I don't know. We'll make do the way we always have."

"I'm going to miss her so much." Julia's grief leaked into her voice.

"I know." He reached for Julia's hand and gently squeezed it. "Alek phoned. He'll be here as soon as he can."

Julia wanted Alek with her. She'd never needed him more. The thought produced another regret. Alek's devotion to her was complete and she deserved so little. She'd treated him terribly and yet he loved her.

Her fears were rampant, fed by her burning tears and broken dreams. Julia felt as though she were being tossed around like a rowboat in a hurricane. Sitting still was impossible; she stood and started pacing.

They sat silently for another hour. Perhaps it was longer, Julia didn't know. She did what she thought might make her grandmother more comfortable. She held Ruth's hand, read her favorite passages from Scripture, smoothed the hair from her brow.

"I have to go." Jerry spoke from behind her.

Understanding, Julia nodded. She loved her brother and knew that he was grieving in his own way. She was grateful he was leaving; she preferred this time alone with Ruth.

"When will you head for home?"

"I don't know yet."

The next thing she heard was the sound of the door closing. It was a relief and a burden. Julia recognized the inconsistency of her thoughts. Her mind seemed to have divided itself. Never had she wanted Alek's company more, and yet she wanted this time alone with her grandmother, sensing that it would be the last time they'd be together.

Julia found it utterly ironic that hope and despair could feel the same to her.

The nurses came in a number of times. One encouraged her to take a break, go have some dinner, but Julia refused. She was afraid to leave, fearing that once she did, her grandmother would quietly release her hold on life.

With her forehead braced against the side of the hospital bed, Julia must have dozed because the next thing she knew Alek was there.

"How is she?"

"There's been no change."

Alek sat down next to Julia. "Have you had dinner?"

"I'm not hungry."

Alek nodded and when he spoke again it was in Russian. The language had a beauty all its own, Julia realized. Whatever he was saying seemed to please her grandmother because Ruth smiled. At first Julia was convinced she had imagined it. It would have been easy enough to do. But there was no denying the change in Ruth's ashen features.

"It's midnight, my love."

Julia glanced at her watch, sure he was mistaken. She must have slept far longer than she realized.

"Come," he said, standing behind her, his hands cupping her shoulders. "I'll drive you home."

She shook her head and resisted, unwilling to leave.

"You aren't doing her any good, and you're running yourself down both physically and mentally."

"You go on ahead," she argued. "I'll stay a little longer."

She heard the frustration in his sigh. "I'm not leaving without you. You're exhausted and irrational."

That sounded like the norm to her.

"I'm afraid to leave her," she whispered brokenly after a while. The time had come for the truth, painful as it was. Julia was surprised she'd chosen to voice it with Alek and not her brother.

"Why?" her husband inquired gently.

She was glad he was standing behind her and couldn't see the tears in her eyes. "If Ruth dies, a part of me will go with her." The best part, Julia feared. Something would perish in her own heart of hearts. Her faith in God and in herself would be shaken and she wondered if the damage would be beyond repair this time.

"Do you wish to bind her to this life, this pain?"

"No," Julia answered honestly. Yet a part of her held on to Ruth fiercely.

A part of Julia had died with her father. It had been joy. Trust had vanished afterward when she realized everything he'd told her about Roger was true. She hadn't wanted to believe her father, had argued with him, fought with him. It was while they were shouting at each other that he'd suffered the heart attack that had prematurely claimed his life.

Joy had faded from her soul that afternoon, replaced by guilt. In the years since she'd made a semi-comfortable life for herself. She wasn't happy, nor was she unhappy. She buried herself in her work, the desire to succeed propelling her forward, dictating her actions. Her goal was to undo the damage Roger had caused the company. First she would rebuild Conrad Industries to its former glory, and then continue on the course her father had so carefully charted.

She was making progress, not only with Conrad Industries, but with her life. Encouraged by Ruth, Julia was just beginning to recapture some of the enthusiasm she'd lost. She could laugh occasionally, even joke every now and again.

It seemed impossible that she would ever again feel anything but the weight of her sadness. Then without being aware of the transformation, she realized she was feeling again, and it had started after her marriage to Alek.

Now here she was again, trapped in the jaws of pain and fear, and it was too soon. Much too soon.

"Come," Alek urged, taking her by the shoulders.

She followed because she hadn't the strength to resist him. Leaning forward, she kissed Ruth's cheek and felt the moisture rain down her own.

Alek gently guided his wife from the hospital room. He kept his arm around her, wanting to lend her his strength. She would never admit she needed him, never confess she was pleased he'd come to be with her. He was at the airport that afternoon, dealing with the Immigration people, working out the final details of his sister's entry into the country. He had been torn between his duty to his sister and Julia needing him.

It was the promise of winning her love that gave him the incentive to continue.

Alek found he was growing weary of this constant battle between them. She fought him at every turn, denied him as her husband. Cheated him out of her love and gentleness. At every turn, she struggled to thwart him. Yet he loved her and was more determined than ever to win her heart.

Instinctively Alek realized that once he scaled her defenses the rarest and most valuable of treasures awaited him. Her love.

He knew only bits and snatches from the past. Even Jerry seemed reluctant to speak of Julia's relationship with Roger Stanhope.

Whenever his friend mentioned the other man's name, Jerry's mouth tightened and anger flashed into his eyes. Because he was so often deeply involved with his own work, Alek wasn't often able to interact with other staff members. Recently he'd made a point to do so.

Over lunch that afternoon, he'd casually dropped Roger Stanhope's name and was amazed at the abrupt silence that fell over the small gathering.

"If you want to know about Roger, just ask Julia," someone suggested.

It sounded like an accusation, which puzzled Alek all the more. From what little he was able to surmise, Roger had been blamed for the fire. But if that was the case, then why wasn't he in jail? Questions abounded. The answers, as so much else in his marriage, would come with time.

Julia was silent on the ride from the hospital to their home. Alek led her into the condo and toward the bedroom where she chose to sleep.

She sat on the edge of the mattress like a lifeless doll propped against the wall.

"Would you like some help undressing?" he asked her gently.

She shook her head. "No, thanks."

He left her, not because he wanted to.

Venturing into the kitchen, he put on a pot of tea. Julia needed something hot and sweet. When the tea had finished steeping, he returned to her room and knocked lightly on the door.

"Come in."

She'd changed clothes and was dressed in a sexless pair of cotton pajamas.

"I made tea." He carried in a cup and saucer and set them on the nightstand next to her bed.

She stared at the cup as if it were something she feared.

"My sister arrived from Prushkin this afternoon. My mother will be free to follow soon, within a couple of months. I was at the airport meeting Anna. That's why I couldn't come to the hospital until late. Anna will be here first thing in the morning."

"Why are you so good to me? I don't deserve it...not after the way I've treated you. Not after the things I've said and done."

He had no answer for her because the truth would only enhance her distress. He loved her as any husband cared for his wife. In time she would recognize and accept his love. But for now she wasn't ready.

Alek peeled back the covers of her bed and fluffed up the pillow. She stood behind him and her breathing grew heavy and labored, as if she was struggling not to weep.

"Alek." His name was a mere whisper. "Would you mind... would you sleep with me tonight? Just this once?"

The ready desire that invaded his body came as more of a shock than her request. From the first night of their marriage Alek had been waiting for her to willingly invite him to her bed. He hadn't imagined it would happen this way, when she was emotionally distraught.

In one and the same instant Alek recognized she wasn't offering him her body. She was seeking out his comfort. It wasn't want he wanted, but it was one small step in the right direction and he was willing to take whatever token Julia offered.

He reached for her hand, kissed her fingers and then moved to the doorway where he switched off the light. Darkness spilled into the room. He heard the mattress squeak as she slipped beneath the sheets. He walked back to the bed, stripped off his clothes and joined her.

It was the sweetest torture he'd ever known to have Julia eagerly scoot into his waiting arms. She cuddled her soft, feminine body against his, molding herself, her satiny smooth leg brushing against his muscled length. She released one long sigh as her head nestled against his chest, and was instantly asleep.

Asleep.

Alek grinned mockingly to himself and wrapped his arm around her shoulders. He listened to the even sound of her breathing and after a few moments, kissed the crown of her head.

So this was to be his lot. Comforter. Not lover or husband, but consoler. His body throbbed with wanting her. To hold her so close was the purest form of torment Alek had ever endured.

He didn't sleep and was grateful he hadn't given in to the respite of slumber, because Julia stirred suddenly, trapped it seemed in the folds of a nightmare. She thrashed around until he managed to hold her down.

"No," she sobbed and twisted away from him. Her long nails dug into his flesh.

"Julia," he whispered, "wake up, it's just a dream."

She raised her head from the pillow, looked into his eyes and frowned. Rubbing a hand over her face, she looked again as though she expected him to have disappeared.

"It's all right," he whispered soothingly. "I'm here."

He could feel her heart throbbing as if she were involved in an aerobic workout. Her eyes met his in the darkness and he read her confusion. It was on the tip of his tongue to remind her she'd invited him into her bed. But he didn't. Instead he plowed his fingers into the thickness of her hair and brought her mouth to his.

She welcomed his kiss without hesitation, without restraint, moaning. She pressed her palms against his chest, then curled her fingers. Her nails were sharp but if this small pain was the price she demanded for loving her, then Alek would pay it willingly.

Her tongue sought out his and a moan of surprise and welcome curled in his throat. Her fingers laced behind his head and her mouth opened his. Their tongues met in a familiar duel.

She sighed when they'd finished kissing. A sigh he recognized well. It spoke of satisfaction, and confusion. And wonder.

His body was on fire, but he didn't press her for more. She snuggled against him and draped her arm around his front and nestled back into their original position. Her hand was restless as it leisurely roamed across his chest, easing away the slight pain she had caused him in her panic from the dream. Her gentleness was a treasure he would lock in his heart to pull out and examine when it seemed there was no hope for them.

Her face angled toward his, her eyes warm and limpid. Alek couldn't resist kissing her again. Tenderly this time. He couldn't force himself to draw too far from her. They were so close, both physically and emotionally, he wanted this moment to go on forever.

A soft lullaby came to Alek then. He didn't have much of a singing voice, but this was a song his mother had sung to him as a child when he was troubled. Julia wouldn't understand the words, but they would soothe her mangled spirit as they had his.

After the first verse, she released a long, trembling sigh. Within a few moments she was sound asleep once more.

Alek followed her shortly.

Julia opened her eyes and felt the unbearable weight of her sadness crushing down on her. Ruth was dying. She rolled over and realized it wasn't grief that was pressing her down, but Alek.

Alek! Her heart went into sudden chaos as she vainly tried to recall the events from the night before. Oh, sweet heaven, she'd asked him…asked him to sleep with her. She'd been distraught. She hadn't known what she was doing and now he'd think, he'd assume she wanted him to make love to her…that she'd welcome him to her bed every night.

Scrambling off the mattress, she backed away from him, her hand at her breast.

"Julia?"

Her heart yo-yoed from her stomach to her throat. She'd hoped to slip away without waking him.

"Good morning."

"'Morning," she said shyly.

"Did you sleep well?"

Julia nodded, and lowered her gaze as the tears sprang readily to the surface.

"Julia?" He reached for her hand, bringing her back to the bed. She sat on the edge of the mattress and he wrapped his arms around her and held her from behind. Words weren't necessary, just then. She was grieving and Alek was there to comfort her, to absorb her pain. She placed her hands over his and their fingers entwined.

"Thank you," she whispered, when she was able to form the words. She leaned back against him, snuggling into his warmth. He kissed her hair and she turned abruptly and looped her arms around his neck, holding him to her for all she was worth.

He spoke to her, and she smiled softly when she realized it was in Russian. He didn't seem to realize she didn't understand him. It didn't matter. She knew what he was saying just by his tone, that he was there, that he loved her.

For the first time, the thought didn't terrify her.

Sometime later, Julia dressed, although she had trouble holding back the tears. She finished before Alek and wandered into the kitchen intent on putting together a pot of coffee. She stopped short when she caught sight of a woman working in her kitchen.

"Good morning," the woman said, struggling with the language. "I'm Anna, Alek's sister."

Chapter Seven

"Hello, Anna." Julia felt like a fool, and blamed Alek for not telling her that his sister had arrived. "Welcome to America."

"Thank you." Alek's sister was small and enviably thin with brown hair woven into a thick plait. Her eyes were so like Alek's that it was as if Julia were staring into her husband's own dark gaze. Her smile was warm and friendly and despite this awkward beginning, Julia liked her immediately.

"My English is poor, but I'm studying every day."

"I'm sure you'll do just fine," Julia said, wondering why Anna was staring at her so intently.

"I'll cook your breakfast."

Although her English was flawless, Anna's accent was so heavy Julia had to struggle to make out some words. "Thank you."

"Eggs and toast?"

"That'll be fine," Julia answered and hurried into the bathroom. By the time she entered the kitchen, she understood Anna's concern. There'd been tears in her eyes and Alek's sister must have assumed they'd been arguing. She hoped to find a way to reassure Anna later that that wasn't the case.

Her breakfast was on the table. Generally Julia ate on the run, usually by picking up a container of orange juice and a muffin at the local convenience store on her way into the office. When Alek had suggested they hire his sister as a housekeeper and cook, Julia had readily agreed. It was a way of helping his family. A way of repaying her debt to him. A way of eating regular meals herself.

It wasn't until she sampled the fluffiest, most delicious scrambled eggs that she'd ever tasted that Julia realized Anna was the one doing her and Alek the favor.

She was reading over the morning newspaper when Alek appeared in the kitchen, smartly dressed. He poured himself a cup of coffee while his sister spoke enthusiastically in her own tongue.

"English," Julia heard him say. "You must speak English."

"This country is so beautiful."

"Yes," Alek agreed, scooting out of the chair and sitting across from Julia, who opted to ignore him. She centered her concentration on the newspaper.

"Did you phone the hospital?" Alek asked.

"Yes...there's been no change. I'm going into the office this morning."

"You'll let me know if you hear anything?"

"Of course."

His gaze locked with hers and he smiled. Julia found herself responding, treasuring this understanding between them, this trust and need they'd stumbled upon. But it frightened her. She wasn't willing to surrender to him, not yet. She held fast to that deep part of herself, and when Alek recognized her reserve, he sighed and mumbled something she couldn't understand.

Anna said something to Alek in Russian. Naturally Julia couldn't understand the words, but it sounded very much as if her sister-in-law was upset with Alek. She offered Julia a sympathetic look as she hurried out the door.

Alek returned his attention to Julia. "She thinks I caused your tears this morning. Let me suffice it to say, she wasn't pleased with me."

"Did you tell her about Ruth?"

"No. She was willing to think ill of me, so I let her. She'll learn the truth soon enough."

"But why would you do that?"

Alek pressed his finger to her lips. "Don't worry about my sister and me. We understand each other."

It was a mistake to go into the office, Julia recognized almost immediately. There were several pressing matters that needed to be taken care of before she spent any more time at the hospital. Appointments to reschedule, work to delegate. Julia resented every minute she spent at her desk. She found herself rushing and impatient to get back to the hospital. Her relationship with Alek concerned her, too.

Sitting at her desk, Julia pressed her face into her hands. She'd been so sure this marriage would never work. Now she wasn't sure of anything. She needed Alek, and he'd come to her, held her, comforted her. For the course of their marriage, she'd given him plenty of reasons to turn away from her. He confronted her with each slight, demanding his rights. When the opportunity came to comfort her, he'd come, willingly, unselfishly.

Each day Julia felt herself weakening a little more, giving in to the attraction she felt for Alek. Every day he found some small way of dismantling the protective wall she'd built around her heart. Brick by brick he was slowly, methodically exposing her to the warming rays of the sun. She'd stood so long in the shadows that she'd grown comfortable with the coolness of the dark.

Julia wanted to stand up and shout that she didn't need a man in her life, didn't want a husband. Silently she did, closing her eyes and forcing him from her mind's eye. But the echo of her cry came back empty.

It was while she was forcing herself not to think of Alek, to concentrate her efforts on the tasks that demanded her attention, that he casually strolled into her office.

"I thought we should talk," he said, plunking himself down in a chair as if he had every right to do so.

"About what?" She pretended to be absorbed in reading her latest batch of correspondence.

"Last night."

He sounded so flippant, so glib, as if their sleeping in the same bed had all been part of his game plan from the beginning. She'd conveniently fallen into his scheme without realizing what she was doing. His attitude infuriated her.

"It was a mistake," she informed him abruptly. "One that won't be repeated."

"It was too much to hope you'd think otherwise," he said with a beleaguered sigh. "If you don't want to accept the truth, then I'll say it for you. It felt good to hold you in my arms, Julia. I'm here if you need me. I'll always be here for you. If you believe nothing else about me, believe this."

Julia felt her chest tighten as he stood and without waiting for her to comment, walked out of her office. She didn't understand this man she'd married, and doubted that she ever would. She'd rewarded his kindness by cheating him, insulting him, and abusing his pride. Not once, but time and again.

Julia didn't want to love Alek. Love frightened her more than any other emotion, even pain. She pulled a little more inside herself, blocking Alek from her heart, because it was only then that she was safe.

Removing the slim gold band from her finger, she stared at it, amazed that something so thin could yield such power. She slipped it back onto her finger, wondering if she'd ever understand Alek, then doubted it was possible when she had yet to understand herself.

It required nearly two hours to clear her desk and her schedule before Julia was free to leave for the hospital.

Her heart grew heavy as she walked down the long, wide corridor that led to her grandmother's room. She didn't stop at the nurses' station, didn't ask to talk to Ruth's physician. Instead she went directly to the woman who'd helped her through the most difficult period of her life.

As Julia silently opened the door and stepped inside, she felt tears burn the back of her eyes. It looked as though her grandmother was asleep. Ruth's face was as pale as alabaster, but she seemed more at peace now, as if the pain had passed.

Tentatively Julia ventured to her grandmother's bedside and gently took her hand in her own. She held it to her own cheek and pressed it there. Slowly Julia closed her eyes.

As soon as she did, it felt as if Ruth were awake, awaiting her arrival so she could speak with her.

Julia had never had much of an imagination, but the figure of her grandmother that formed in her mind didn't shock or frighten her. If she were to seek an excuse, Julia would attribute it to her exhausted mental state.

"Don't be sad," Ruth seemed to be saying to her. "I don't want you to grieve for me. I've lived a good, long life. You were my joy. God's special gift to me."

"No, please," Julia pleaded silently. "Don't leave me, please don't leave."

"Julia, my child. You have your whole life ahead of you. Don't cling to the past. Look instead to the future. You have a husband who adores you and children waiting to be born. Your life is just beginning. So much love awaits you, more joy that you can bear to know about now. Your pain shall reap an abundant bouquet of life's treasure. Trust me in this."

"Treasures," Julia whispered. She couldn't look past the moment to think about the future. It was impossible when her heart was breaking.

Tears ran unrestrained down her face and she felt her grandmother's presence reaching out to comfort her, to soothe her soul, a last farewell before she set out on the journey that lay before her.

Julia didn't know how long she stood, holding on to Ruth's hand. She realized as she looked up at the monitor registering her grandmother's heart rate that it had gone silent. Ruth had quietly slipped from life into death with no fuss, no ceremony, as if she'd been awaiting Julia's arrival so she could peacefully leave.

Julia knew it would be impossible to emotionally prepare herself for this moment. She'd been right. Ruth's death wasn't a shock; she'd been ill for years. Each day, Julia realized, could be her grandmother's last. She'd accepted the inevitability of Ruth's passing as best she could. But nothing could have prepared her for the sledgehammer of grief that slammed against her heart. Nothing.

Collapsing into the chair, Julia's cry came in a low, grief-filled wail as she swayed back and forth.

A nurse arrived, a doctor and several other health professionals. Julia didn't move. She couldn't. The sobs racked her shoulders and she buried her face in her hands. And slowly rocked with her grief.

Someone wrapped a pair of arms around her and led her from the room. She sat in the private area, alone, desolate, inconsolable.

Jerry and Alek arrived together. Jerry spoke with the hospital officials while Alek gently wrapped Julia in his arms and held her against him as she wept until there were no more tears in the well of her pain.

She needed him and was past pretending she didn't. Her own strength was depleted. Clinging to Alek, she buried her face in his chest and sought what solace she could. When her father had died, she'd been numb with guilt and grief. The tears hadn't come until much later.

He held her close and she was so grateful for his comfort that she tried to burrow closer, thinking he would somehow absorb her grief.

It seemed they were at the hospital for hours. There were papers to sign and a hundred different decisions to be made. Jerry went with her and Alek to the funeral home where the arrangements were made for Ruth's burial.

Julia was surprised with the calm, almost unemotional way she was able to deal with the mundane details of the funeral. The flowers, the music, discussing the program with first the funeral home director and then with the family's minister, Pastor Hall.

It was dark by the time they'd finished. Jerry, solemn and pale, walked out to the parking lot with her and Alek.

"Do you want to come back to the condo with us?" Julia asked, not wanting to leave her brother alone. Unlike her, he'd return to an empty house. Ruth's death had badly shaken him. He didn't express his grief as freely as she had.

Jerry shook his head. "No, thanks."

"Anna has dinner ready and waiting," Alek supplied.

"I'll pick up something on the way home," he assured them both. "Don't worry about me."

Alek drove through the hilly streets that led to their condominium. "How are you feeling?" he asked, when he opened the front door for her.

"Drained." A truckload of emotions seemed to be pressing against her chest. She was mentally and physically exhausted, as though she'd spent the past eighteen hours involved in some endurance marathon. Her fatigue was so great she could barely hold up her head.

Alek guided her into the kitchen. She hadn't eaten since breakfast, hadn't thought about food even once. The smells were heavenly, but she had no appetite.

Alek brought two plates from the oven and set them down on the table.

"I'm not hungry," she told him. "I'm going to take a bath." She half expected him to argue with her, to insist she needed nourishment. Instead he realized she knew what was best for herself right now, and she was grateful.

One look in the bathroom mirror confirmed Julia's worst suspicions. Her eyes were red, puffy and her cheeks were pale, her makeup long since washed away with her tears. She looked much older than her twenty-seven years. About a hundred years older. She looked and felt as if she'd been hit by a freight train. In some ways she had—an emotional one.

Ruth was gone and other than Jerry she was alone in the world. She was grateful for Alek's assistance this traumatic day, but in time he would leave and then she'd be alone all over again.

Running her bathwater, she added a package of peach-scented salts and slipped into the hot, soothing water. She leaned against the back of the tub and closed her eyes, letting the heat of the bath comfort her.

Children waiting to be born.

She didn't know why the phrase edged its way back into her mind. There would be no children because there would be no real marriage. She was more determined than ever not to cross that line, especially now, when she was most vulnerable. She'd hurt Alek enough, abused his gentleness, taken advantage of his kindness. She couldn't, wouldn't mislead him into believing there could ever be anything permanent between them.

Her husband was standing in the hallway outside the bathroom waiting for her when she finished. "I'm fine, Alek," she said, wanting to assure him, even if it wasn't entirely true.

"You're exhausted. I turned back the sheets for you."

"Thank you."

He led her into the bedroom as if she were a child. In other circumstances Julia would have resented the way he'd taken control of her life, but not then. Instead she was grateful.

She slipped beneath the sheets, nestled her head against the pillow and closed her eyes. "Alek," she whispered, sensing he remained with her.

"Yes, my love."

"Would you sing to me again?"

He complied with a haunting melody in his own language. His voice was clear and strong and even though she couldn't understand the words, she found it beautiful and soothing. She wanted to ask him the meaning, but her thoughts and her mind drifted in another direction, toward rest. Toward peace.

Julia woke with a start. She didn't know what it was that had jarred her awake. The room was surrounded by darkness and the digital clock on the nightstand informed her it was nearly 1:00 a.m. As her eyes adjusted to the lack of light, she realized Alek was sitting beside her in a chair, his back braced against the wall. His legs were stretched out before him and his head cocked at an odd, uncomfortable angle.

"Alek?" she whispered, leveling herself up on one elbow.

He stirred immediately, abruptly sitting up. His gaze shot to her. "Julia?"

"What are you doing here?"

"I didn't want to leave you alone."

"I'm fine." She wasn't, not really, but was determined not to let him know that.

"Do you want me to sing you to sleep again?"

Hot, burning tears filled her eyes at the tenderness of his concern. She shook her head. What she needed was to be held, to be consoled.

"Julia, my love," he whispered, transferring himself from the chair to the edge of the mattress. His hand smoothed the hair from her face, his touch as gentle as if she were a child badly in need of reassurance. It was exactly the way Julia felt.

"Why do you have to be so damn wonderful?" she sobbed accusingly. "Why are you so good to me?"

His lips touched her brow. "You'll know the answer to that soon enough."

"I'm a rotten wife."

He laughed. "You haven't given yourself a chance yet."

"I've treated you abominably. You should hate me."

"Hate you?" He seemed to find her words amusing. "It would be impossible."

"Will you sleep with me? Please?" The words were out before she could censor the wisdom of asking. It was a completely selfish request. "I...need you, Alek." This last bit was for honesty's sake, to ease her conscience.

He kissed her gently, his mouth unerringly locating hers in the dark. Although his kiss was gentle and light, she knew it was his way of thanking her for admitting the truth.

He stood and stripped off his pants and shirt. Julia lifted the covers and scooted as far as she could to allow him ample space.

After sleeping in his embrace the night before, she felt strangely shy now. He wrapped his arm around her shoulders and brought her close to his side. He was warm and real and felt so alive that she trembled when she pressed her head to his chest. His heart was pounding strong and steady against her ear and she found the cadence strangely relaxing.

"Can you sleep now?"

"I . . . think so. What about you?"

"I'll be fine."

That didn't answer her question, but she didn't press him. "We kissed last night, didn't we?"

He rubbed his chin across the top of her head. "Yes." She heard the strain in his voice and felt unusually pleased. She rotated her head back so that she was looking into his warm, dark eyes. Their breaths merged and mingled. His was warm and moist and thick and her own was soft and irregular. Only a few inches separated their mouths.

"Would you . . . mind—" she hesitated and moistened her lips "—kissing me again?"

His breathing stopped abruptly and his eyes, so dark and gentle, narrowed as if he wasn't sure he should trust her. Julia didn't blame him.

Rather than waiting for his permission, she arched upward toward him until their lips met. Their kiss was sweet and tender, undemanding. She was breathing hard when he finished, but then so was he.

He kissed her again, a little deeper, a little more intensely. Then a lot more intensely.

Julia sighed as his mouth left her, their bottom lips clinging momentarily. "Oh, Alek." She sighed. Closing her eyes, she allowed a trembling kind of response to work its way down her body.

She said his name again, softer this time, heavy with need. "I want to make love."

It seemed as if all the air had been sucked from the room. She watched him closely and noted the wide display of emotions flashing in and out of his eyes. He wanted her, too, she couldn't doubt it. The evidence of his need was pressed against her thigh and refused to be ignored. He wanted her and had from the first day of their marriage. He made certain she knew how much. Yet he hesitated.

His eyes gradually changed and told her another story. They darkened with doubt, which won over the needy, sensual look she'd read in him seconds earlier.

"Julia." He breathed her name and it sounded heavy with regret. "Not now."

"Why not?" She knew she sounded defensive and couldn't help it. He'd been throwing the issue of her being his wife at her from the beginning. He'd demanded that she share his bed from the first night of their marriage.

Yet when she agreed to fulfill her end of their agreement, he rejected her. It made no sense. If anything, it angered her.

"I'd feel as if I was taking advantage of you."

"Shouldn't I be the judge of that?" she said irritably.

"Right now, no."

Stunned, she jerked her head away. Her heart tightened into a painful knot. His fingers came to her face, resting on her cheek, directing her gaze back to his.

"I want you, Julia, don't ever doubt that." Reaching for her hand, he lowered it beneath the covers and pressed her palm over the heat of his erection. "Feel how much."

Her fingers flexed around the strength of his arousal and, groaning, he snatched her hand away. "But I refuse to put my own needs before yours. You're confused and hurting. There's nothing I'd like more than to bury myself so deep inside you—" He stopped and breathed hard once. "I'm sure you understand."

She nodded.

He kissed her briefly and then tucked his arm around her and brought her closer to his side. His lips were in her hair. "When we make love, I don't want there to be any regrets in the morning."

Julia smiled and kissed his bare chest. "No one told me you were so damn noble."

"No one told me, either," he muttered disparagingly under his breath.

The way he said it with a deep, shuddering sigh led her to believe if anyone had regrets in the morning, it would be her husband.

Content now, she nestled against him and closed her eyes. She'd prefer it if they made love, but his holding her would satisfy her for now.

* * *

Alek envied Julia her ability to sleep. Such luxury was to be denied him. For weeks he'd been waiting for his wife to come to him, to willingly fulfill her wedding vows. For weeks his patience with her had been growing thin. Her determination to thwart him had served to tighten his own resolve. Yet when she invited him to her bed, held her arms all soft and tempting around him, he felt compelled to do the honorable thing.

Honor. But at what price? His body throbbed with need. His heart ached with love. No woman had led him on a finer chase. No woman had challenged him as much as his wife. No woman had defied and infuriated him more than Julia.

She'd been hurt and angry at his refusal, then seemed to accept the wisdom of his words. Wisdom, nothing, he was a damned fool.

Maybe not, he decided after a moment. Perhaps he was a wise fool. Only time would tell.

He felt Julia stir some time later and was surprised to realize it was morning. Slowly he opened his eyes to discover her face gazing down on his, studying him. "Good morning," she whispered.

He waited, thinking she might be furious at finding him in bed with her, but she revealed none of the outrage she had the morning before. But her eyes were clouded and her grief was evident.

"Did you sleep well?" he asked.

She nodded shyly, her gaze avoiding his. "What about you?"

"As well as can be expected." He stretched his cramped arms and loudly yawned. They were fools, the pair of them. His sister had said as much yesterday morning. They were sleeping in a single bed, practically on top of each other, when there was a perfectly good king-size bed in the other room.

Alek didn't have a single excuse to offer his sister and finally told her to mind her own damn business. But Anna was right.

"Thank you, Alek," Julia said, climbing out of bed. Her face was turned away from him, he noted.

"For what, sleeping with you?"

"No... well, yes, that, too, but for... you know, not..."

"Making love to you?"

She nodded. Reaching inside her closet, she took out a set of clothes and held them in front of her as if to shield her body from his view. She's spent the majority of the night cuddling against him. He'd felt every inch of her creamy smooth skin; there wasn't anything left to hide. It didn't seem right to point that out, however.

"The next few days are going to be very busy. I'll be spending the majority of my time finishing up the funeral arrangements and... and going through Ruth's things, so we probably won't be seeing much of each other for a while."

She didn't need to sound so genuinely pleased at the prospect, Alek mused.

By the time he'd showered and dressed, Julia had already left the condominium. His sister was eyeing him as though he were a wife beater, clearly displeased about something.

"What's wrong with Julia?" Anna demanded. "She looks as if she was crying."

Naturally it would be his fault, Alek mused, ignoring his sister's glare.

"Her grandmother died," he explained and he watched as Anna's accusing eyes went soft with sympathy.

"You love this woman."

"She's my wife." He saw now that it was a mistake to have hired his sister. It was apparent she was going to be what Jerry called a damned nuisance.

"You did not marry her for love."

"No," he admitted gruffly, disliking this line of questioning. He wouldn't have accepted it from anyone else and Anna knew it.

"She knows that you did not love her. This is why she sleeps in the small bed."

"Thank you, Dear Abby."

"Who?"

"Never mind," Alek said impatiently. He grabbed a piece of toast from the plate and didn't wait for the rest of his breakfast.

"Aleksandr," she said sharply, stopping him. "You've become very American." Her features relaxed into a wide smile. "I think this is good. You teach me, too, okay?"

"Okay," he said, chuckling.

Sorting through Ruth's possessions proved to be far more difficult than Julia had anticipated. Her grandmother's tastes had been simple, but she had held on to several items, refusing to discard life's little mementos.

Disposing of her clothes was the easiest. Julia boxed them up and took them to a shelter for the homeless. It was the little things she found so difficult. A token from the Seattle World's Fair, an empty perfume bottle that had long since faded from the store shelves. The pictures. She could never part with the pictures.

Julia had no idea her grandmother had collected so many snapshots. The comical photos Ruth sent her Louis Conrad while he was away fighting in the Second World War were the ones that made her laugh.

Julia found a packet of pictures that caused her to giggle outright. Her grandmother, so young and attractive, was poised in a modest-looking swimsuit, in front of a photograph of a young soldier. It had to have been Julia's grandfather, but she'd never seen pictures of him at that age.

The whole thing must have been rather risqué for the time. Julia guessed Ruth had been giving Louis a reason to come home. Heaven knew it had worked.

Julia held the picture to her breast and sat for several moments remembering the love story Ruth had told her. It was so sweet and innocent, unlike modern times when sex dominated a relationship.

Not her marriage, she noted, defeatedly. It was difficult to believe that she could have been married to Alek this long without them making love.

He'd been eager for the physical side of their relationship, until she'd revealed the first signs of wanting him, too. How very typical of a man. Julia found herself smiling. It had been so long since she'd laughed that her face muscles began to ache.

"Oh, Alek," she breathed, holding her grandmother's picture to her breast. "Will there ever be a way for us?"

In her heart was a resounding *yes*. But the voice wasn't her own, nor was it Alek's. It came from Ruth.

* * *

The day of the funeral, Julia donned a black dress and a pillbox hat with a black netting that fitted over her face. She dreaded this ritual from the first and was grateful that Jerry and Alek had seen to the majority of the details.

Julia hadn't slept well the past few nights and the fatigue was beginning to show. She'd made a point of coming home late, knowing Alek would be waiting for her. She'd mumble something about being tired and closing her bedroom door, slipped into bed alone.

It was a mistake to boot Alek out of her bed. She spent the past two nights wishing he were there with her. She cursed her foolish pride for not seeking him out. But she was afraid that once she did, she'd ask him to make love to her again and this time she wouldn't take no for an answer.

The limousine delivered Julia, Jerry and Alek to the Methodist church where Ruth had worshiped for several years. Jerry and Alek climbed out first. Alek offered her his hand as Julia stepped out of the car. A small group of mourners formed on the sidewalk outside the church, awaiting the family's arrival. Julia's gaze quickly scanned the crowd, then stopped abruptly.

There seeking her eyes stood Roger Stanhope.

Chapter Eight

Julia hesitated, one foot on the street curb, the other in the limousine. Crouched as she was, she felt in danger of collapsing. Roger had dared to show up at her grandmother's funeral. The man had no sense of decency, but that didn't come as any surprise.

Although Alek couldn't have known what was happening to her, he leaned forward, wrapped his arm around her waist and assisted her to an upright position.

His eyes were filled with concern. Rightly so. Julia's heart was beating at double-time and her head was spinning. She honestly believed she might faint.

"I . . . I need to sit down."

"Of course." With his hand tucked securely around her waist, Alek led her inside the church vestibule. A row of wooden pews lined the wall and Alek gently guided her there.

"What's wrong?" Jerry asked.

For the life of her Julia couldn't answer. "Water . . . could you get me a glass of water?"

Jerry hurried away and returned a moment later with her request. Other friends were beginning to arrive and after taking a few moments to compose herself, Julia stood.

How dare Roger show up for her grandmother's funeral! He'd done it on purpose to agitate her and his unscrupulous ploy had worked. Julia had never been so close to passing out. Not even the day her father had . . . she pushed the thought from her mind, refusing to dwell on anything that had to do with Roger.

Jerry's gaze caught sight of their former employee and his mouth thinned with irritation. "You saw him, didn't you?"

Julia nodded.

"I'll have him thrown out."

"Don't," she said. Roger wasn't worth the effort. "He'll be sure to cause a scene, besides I think Ruth would have gotten a kick out of it. We tried everything but a subpoena to talk to him after the fire, remember?"

"I'm not likely to forget."

"Who would have believed he'd end up coming to us?"

"Not me," Jerry agreed.

Alek didn't say anything, but Julia was well aware of his presence at her side. She wasn't fooled; he took in every word of the exchange between her and her brother.

"Point out this man to me," Alek said to them both. "I will see to his removal."

Jerry's gaze sought out Julia's, looking for her consent. She thought about it a moment, then decided she wouldn't give Roger the satisfaction. His power to wound her had died years earlier.

"Don't kid yourself, Julia, he's up to something," Jerry warned.

"I'd be a fool if I didn't know that," she returned testily. She'd been duped by Roger once and it wasn't a mistake she cared to repeat. She knew his methods and wouldn't be taken in a second time.

The three of them had gathered in the back of the church and were unaware of anyone else until Pastor Hall approached them and announced they were ready for the service to begin.

Julia had anticipated the emotional drain the ordeal would cause. Several times during the funeral she felt close to tears, but she held them at bay, taking in deep, even breaths and nibbling on her lower lip. Her fingers were entwined with Alek's and she appreciated more than ever that he was with her. His presence lent her the strength she needed to get through this heartrending ordeal of saying goodbye to the woman she loved so dearly.

From the church they traveled to the north end of Seattle to the cemetery where Ruth was to be buried in the plot next to her beloved Louis.

Julia was surprised by how many people came. The day was bright and clear and the sky was a pale shade of blue she'd only seen in the Pacific Northwest.

There were so many lovely bouquets of flowers. The group of mourners gathered under the canopy at the cemetery. Julia, Jerry and Alek were given seats, along with a few of Ruth's more elderly friends. Pastor Hall read from his Bible and the words were familiar ones since Julia had read them so often to Ruth herself.

Her heart felt as if it would shatter into a thousand pieces as the casket was slowly lowered into the ground. Alek must have sensed her distress because he placed his arm around her shoulders. The tears sprang from her eyes and she silently sobbed her last farewell to her grandmother.

The assembly met afterward at Ruth's home. Charles, who'd been with the family for years, had insisted upon having it there, although it demanded extra work on his part. The meal was catered, but several friends brought dishes themselves. A wide variety of casseroles, salads and sliced meats were available.

Julia and Jerry stood at the doorway and greeted each caller, thanking them for their love and support. Julia received countless hugs.

Several family friends recounted stories involving Ruth and Louis and before she realized what was happening, Julia found herself smiling. Her grandmother had been a wonderful, generous, warm-hearted woman. It wasn't necessary for Julia to hear it from others for her to recognize the truth, but it reaffirmed what she'd always known.

The gathering broke up into small groups of mourners. Every available seat was taken in the living room and formal dining room. Julia accepted the role of hostess and saw to the guests' comforts.

She was filling coffee cups when Roger spoke from behind her. "Hello, Julia."

It was fortunate that she didn't empty the steaming coffee into someone's lap. Roger had apparently sneaked into the house through the back way, because Jerry would never have allowed him in the front door.

"Hello, Roger," she said as unemotionally as she could.

"I'm sorry to hear about your grandmother."

"Thank you." Her words were civil, if not her tone.

"Julia, Julia," he said with an injured sigh, "isn't it time for us to let bygones be bygones? How many times do I have to tell you it was all a horrible mistake? It seems a shame to rehash something that happened so long ago, don't you agree?"

"I'm sure it wasn't a mistake. Now, if you'll excuse me, I'll see to my guests."

Roger surprised her by taking hold of her arm and stopping her. Her gaze flew back to him and she wondered what it was that she'd ever seen in him. It nauseated her that she could have ever thought herself in love with him.

He was devilishly handsome, but his good looks were so transparent that she was amazed she hadn't seen through his guise much sooner. She'd learned a good deal about character in the past few years, and the thought comforted her.

"I suggest you let go of my wife's arm." Alek's words rang like a hammer against steel.

He was angry. Julia could tell by how heavy his accent became. The words were almost indistinguishable.

Roger looked puzzled, as if he didn't understand.

"I suggest you do as he says," Julia said. Roger purposely chose to misinterpret Alek's words, but he hadn't fooled her.

Roger released her arm. He held up both hands for Alek's inspection. "I heard you'd married," he said, continuing to follow her as she filled yet another coffee cup. Alek came after Roger and the three of them paraded across the room.

"Why you chose to marry a Russian is beyond me. I thought you were smarter than to involve yourself with some foreigner."

Julia didn't give the comment the dignity of a reply. Instead she introduced the two men. "Roger Stanhope, meet Aleksandr Berinski."

"Ah," Roger said sarcastically, "and I thought he was your bodyguard."

"I am," Alek said in a less heavier accent. "Touch my wife again and I'll show you how excruciating a broken arm can be. We foreigners have effective ways of causing much pain."

"Alek," Julia admonished with a grin.

Roger seemed to take the threat as some kind of joke. "I'm truly sorry to hear about your grandmother," he continued.

"Thank you." The coffeepot was empty and Julia returned to the kitchen with both Roger and Alek in tow. If it hadn't been so sad an occasion, Julia would have found the antics of the two men hilarious.

"I'd like to take you to lunch sometime," Roger continued, leaning against the kitchen counter as Julia assembled another pot of coffee. "We could talk over old times."

"Great. I'd love it. Do you mind if I bring the chief who investigated the fire?"

"Julia won't be having lunch with you," Alek answered unevenly.

"I'm sorry, Roger, really I am, but my husband is the jealous sort. You've started off on the wrong foot with him as it is, I suggest you don't press your luck."

"Julia, sweetheart," Roger said with a meaningful sigh, "it's time for us to clear the air."

"The air will be much clearer once you leave," Alek intervened. "Perhaps you would allow me to show you to the door?"

"Ah . . ." Roger wasn't given a chance to reply. Julia couldn't see what it was Alek did, but Roger's eyes bulged and he arched his back and nodded. "All right, sure, I'll leave."

"I thought you'd see matters my way," Alek said with a roguish grin.

Roger relaxed and cast an ugly look in Alek's direction. He straightened the cuffs of his starched white shirt and wore an injured air as he vacated the house through the back door.

Julia's gaze followed Roger. "That wasn't really necessary, you know."

"Ah, but it gave me a good deal of pleasure."

Her smiling eyes met his. "Me, too."

"Tell me about this man. You loved him?"

The amusement drained from her face like water sucked down a bathtub drain. She was surprised no one had ever told Alek about her and Roger's fateful relationship. She'd dealt with enough grief for one day and wasn't interested in delving into more.

"Another time?" she asked.

Alek seemed to require some time to think over his answer. "Soon," he told her. "A husband needs to know these things."

She agreed with a short, unenthusiastic nod.

Alek was leaving the kitchen when she stopped him. "I'll tell you about Roger if you tell me about the women in your life."

This too seemed to give him pause. "There's never been anyone but you," he said, and then grinned boyishly.

The gathering broke up sometime later. Julia insisted upon staying and helping Charles with the necessary cleanup. Jerry and Alek were helpful, too, dismantling folding chairs, straightening the living room and carrying dirty dishes into the kitchen.

By the time Alek unlocked the door to their home, Julia was physically and mentally exhausted.

"Sit down," Alek instructed, "and I'll make you a cup of tea."

"That sounds heavenly." She kicked off her shoes and stretched her tired legs across the ottoman. Alek joined her a few minutes later, carrying a china cup and saucer.

He sat across from her.

"I don't think I'll ever stop missing her," Julia whispered, after her first tentative sip of tea. Now that she wasn't so busy, the pain of losing Ruth returned full force. "She's left such a large void."

"Give yourself time," Alek offered gently.

Julia looked over to her husband and her heart swelled with an unnamed emotion. Possibly love. The thought frightened her half to death, but with Alek there was the chance of feeling safe and secure again.

He'd been so good to her through the strain of Ruth's illness and death, even when she'd given him ample reason to be angry with her.

"When was the last time you ate?" he asked her unexpectedly.

Julia had to think. "I don't remember."

"You didn't have anything this afternoon."

"I didn't?" There'd been so much food, it seemed impossible that she hadn't eaten something herself.

"No," Alek informed her. "I was watching. You saw to everyone else but yourself. I'll cook you dinner myself."

"Alek, please," she said, following him into the kitchen. "This isn't necessary."

"It'll be my pleasure." Taking hold of her by the waist, he effortlessly lifted her onto the stool next to the kitchen counter. "You can stay and watch," he said. "You might even learn something."

Relaxed now, Julia smiled.

Alek looked at her for several moments. "You don't do that often enough," he said, leaning toward her and gently planting a kiss on her lips, surprising her.

"Do what?"

"Smile."

"There hasn't been much reason to."

"That's about to change, my love."

She propped her chin up between her hands. The sadness she'd carried with her all these weeks seemed to slide off her back. "You know, I think you're right."

Alek, who was whipping up a couple of eggs, looked over to her and grinned. "Anna said something to me the other morning. As her older brother I'm guilty of not listening to my sister as often as I should. This time, I know she's right."

"I like Anna very much."

"She feels the same way about you. She told me you were wise not to let me make love to you."

Julia lowered her gaze, growing uncomfortable with his choice of topics.

"When we married I wasn't in love with you," Alek confessed. "You weren't in love with me. This is true?"

Given no option but the truth, Julia nodded.

"My heart tells me differently now." He set the bowl aside and moved to her side. Pressing his finger beneath her chin, he raised her eyes so they were level with his own. "I love you, Julia, very much."

She bit into her trembling lower lip. "Oh, Alek..." Tears gathered in her eyes until the vision of his sweet face swam before her.

"This makes you sad?"

"This terrifies me. I want to love you...I think I already do, but I don't trust myself when it comes to falling in love."

Alek frowned. "Because of this weak man you saw today?"

"Roger? Yes, because of Roger."

"I am not this man."

"I know." In her head she realized as much, but her heart was having trouble telling the difference.

Alek slipped his arms around her middle and Julia was struck not for the first time by the incredible beauty she saw in him. Not the physical kind. Oh, he was handsome enough, but that wasn't what captured her attention. She saw the man who had held and comforted her when her grandmother had died. The man who had sung her to sleep. The man who refused to take advantage of her even when she'd asked him to do so.

They stared at each other for what seemed like an eternity.

Julia knew the moment Alek decided to make love to her. It was the same moment she realized she'd die if he didn't.

His mouth sought hers in a hungry kiss. "I love you," he whispered against her lips.

"I love you, too," she echoed, so lost in his kiss that she couldn't speak anything but the truth. She'd tried to fool herself into believing it wasn't possible to trust a man again. Alek was different, he had to be. If she couldn't trust him, then there was no hope for her.

His arms gripped her waist as he lifted her from the stool. Her feet dangled several inches off the floor as he carried her out of the kitchen and into the bedroom, kissing her, nibbling at her lips as he progressed across the condominium.

Julia lolled her head back in an effort to gather her scattered wits. Her breath came in disruptive bursts, her lungs empty of air. Feeling was more important than breathing. Alek's touch, which was most important of all, brought back to life the desire that had lain dormant in her for years.

He laid her across the king-size mattress and joined her there, his mouth eating away at hers, revealing sensual mysteries with his lips and tongue. He was sprawled across her, pinning her to the bed.

"You're so beautiful," he whispered. "You make me crazy." He buried his tongue in her mouth, to be met by her own in a passionate play between them.

"Love me," she told him, her arms around his neck. She felt safe with Alek. Safe with herself and her judgment.

"I do love you, always." He lowered his mouth to hers. His kiss was sweet and gentle as his hands fiddled with the zipper in the back of her dress. Growing impatient, he rolled her onto her side, turning with her in order to ease the fastening open. He removed the dress, along with her silk top, panty hose and tap pants.

He ran his hand up and down her bare thighs, over her buttocks to the dip at the small of her back. "You're so soft," he said, his voice filled with awe.

Julia buried her face in the thick cord of his neck. "You're so hard."

"You noticed."

"I couldn't help it."

Easing his hands over her stomach, he splayed his fingers across her abdomen. He didn't speak but Julia knew he was thinking forward to the time she would carry his child, nestled beneath her heart. His thoughts were an echo of her own.

His hand wandered lower, to the downy softness at the portal of her womanhood. He hesitated only a moment, tested her moistness before he dipped his finger inside her dewy warmth. His touch was tentative, as though he was afraid of hurting her. Sensation bubbled and churned inside her, rushing like a hot river through the lower half of her body.

Bracing her hands against his shoulders, Julia closed her eyes and buckled. She was hot and tight and a painful, heavy throbbing moved through her.

"Alek." She didn't know what she wanted, only that she wanted, and the need was desperate. She wrapped her arms around his neck and kissed him with a hunger that bordered on the wild. As she moved, her bare breasts brushed against him. Her erect nipples stabbed at his chest. Until then she hadn't realized he still had on his clothes. She eagerly worked at the buttons of his shirt, peeling it open and splaying her fingers across his muscled strength.

He worked at his belt buckle, disrupting their foreplay for a moment while he shed the remainder of his clothing. Everything went with the exception of his tie, which seemed to require more hassle than he had patience to deal with.

Julia was on her back watching him. "Leave it, it's very sexy," she said, reaching for the end and pulling him back to her.

Alek positioned himself above her and she spread her thighs, welcoming him. Opening her body and her heart. Opening her life. She closed her eyes to the gentle probing pressure of his entry.

As he filled her, Julia sighed at the intense pleasure she experienced and her low moan mingled with his. She gasped at the wild sensation that shot through her at his slow, deep movements.

Alek stopped at the sound of her pleasure. "I'm too big for you."

"No... no, don't stop. Alek, please."

He eased his weight forward, thrusting more deeply into her. His hands gripped her hips, leveling her buttocks from the mattress.

Feeling, wild and hot, exploded inside her and she gasped and jerked her hips wildly. Alek soon reached his own satisfaction and cried out her name in his pleasure.

Together their breaths came in the same scattered rhythm.

Neither spoke. Alek repeatedly kissed her as Julia silently wept. These were tears of jubilation, tears of joy. Her season of pain had passed just as her grandmother had claimed it would. She'd found her joy in Alek.

It was as though the past three years of Julia's life had been a nightmare. With her husband's arms wrapped around her, his kiss on her lips, her sated body smothered by his, Julia felt as though the nightmare had slipped away. She was whole again because of Alek. Complete. Loved and loving.

The sobs returned as she spread soft kisses over his face. "I love you," she chanted. "Thank you, oh, thank you."

He spoke to her in his language and Julia guessed he was thanking her, too.

They slept, their arms wrapped around each other, their bodies cuddling spoon-fashion. Alek tucked his leg over hers and pressed close to her backside.

Julia woke first, hungry and loving. She rolled over so that her head was nestled beneath Alek's chin. Using her tongue, she created a moist highway on the underside of his jaw.

"Hmm."

"You awake?"

"I am now," he muttered drowsily.

"I'm hungry. Do you want to order out for dinner?"

Alek grinned. "I was going to cook for us, remember?"

Julia scooted closer, wrapping her arms around his neck, delving her fingers into his thick head of hair. "I think you should conserve your strength for later," she advised, bringing his mouth down to hers.

* * *

Gentle flames flickered over the gas logs in Julia's fireplace while they lounged on the floor, a boxed pizza resting nearby on the plush, light gray carpeting. Alek had found a bottle of wine and poured them each a glass.

"You're quiet," Alek commented.

Julia leaned back her head and smiled up at him. They couldn't seem to be apart from each other, even for a moment. Not just then. His touch was her reality.

His arms tightened around her. "Any regrets?"

"None."

He kissed the side of her neck. "Me, either."

"I thought you'd gloat. Our making love is a real feather in your cap."

His hand crept between the opening in her robe and cupped her breast. "I care nothing for feathers. All I want is my wife." He stroked his chin across the top of her head. "Are you still hungry?"

Julia patted her stomach. "Not a bit. Are you?"

"Yes. I'm half-starved, I fear."

The odd catch in his voice told her it wasn't food that interested him. He went still, as though he feared her response. Looking up at him, she stared into his deep, dark eyes and slowly, carefully smiled. "I have a feeling I've awakened a monster," she teased.

Alek pressed her down into the thick carpet, his eyes seeking hers. "Do you mind?"

"No," she whispered, untying the sash to her silk robe, "I don't mind in the least."

Alek's mouth was moving down to hers when the phone rang. He froze and so did Julia.

"Let it ring," she suggested, rubbing her hands over his chest, loving the smooth feel of his skin.

"It could be important." Reluctantly his eyes moved from her to the phone.

"You're probably right," Julia muttered, although she was far more interested in making love with her husband than talking on the phone.

"I'll get it." He scrambled across the floor on all fours and reached for the receiver. "Hello," he said impatiently.

Julia followed behind, kneeling beside him. Leaning forward, she caught his ear lobe between her teeth and sucked gently.

"Hello, Jerry," he said meaningfully.

Julia playfully progressed from his ear to his chin, then down the side of his neck, using her tongue to create a moist trail. The bulge in Alek's shorts told her how successful her attentions to details were.

"Yes, Julia's right here." He sounded winded, as if he was under a good deal of strain.

Julia intended to increase that strain tenfold. She eased her hand past the elastic waistband of his briefs and went on her own private mission. He caught her by the wrist, stopping her. His eyes were snapping at her and Julia couldn't help it, she laughed out loud.

"It's for you."

She lowered her gaze to the large swelling in his front. "I know."

"I mean the phone."

Julia reached for the receiver, her eyes holding Alek's. "Hello, Jerry," she said in a clear, even voice. "You caught me at a bad moment, something's come up. Would you mind if I called you back in say...twenty minutes?''

"Ah...sure." Her brother wasn't pleased, but that couldn't be helped.

"Thanks." She set the phone back on its cradle, then changed her mind and removed the headpiece.

"Something's come up?" Alek quizzed, struggling to hide a smile.

"Most definitely. Something very important."

Alek's hand slid upward over her abdomen to capture her generous breast. Julia bit into her lip when he began to stroke the nipple with the side of his thumb.

It hardened in ready response and the naked need braided its way through her body. "Alek." Once again she found herself pleading with him.

Grinning, Alek cupped her breast in one hand and lifted it as if in offering, then lowered his mouth, sucking until she twisted and bucked against the floor.

He was greedy but gentle, stopping only once, just long enough to tell her he didn't think twenty minutes would be near enough time.

Alek was right. Nearly forty minutes passed before Julia returned her brother's phone call.

"Hello, Jerry," she said, when he answered the phone. "I'm sorry I'm late."

"You should be. What the hell is going on over there, anyway? I've been trying to call you for the past fifteen minutes and all I could get was a busy signal."

"Sorry, but we were busy."

The pause that followed was significant. "Ah. I see. So," he said smugly, "how do you like married life now?"

"I like it just fine." It embarrassed her to be discussing her love life with her brother even in the most innocent of ways. "I take it your call was important."

"Yes, it is." Jerry's voice sharpened. "It's about Roger."

Julia groaned inwardly. Would she never be rid of the man? "What's he up to now?"

"I told you he was after something when he showed up for the funeral."

"We both know he didn't come out of respect," Julia agreed.

"I got a call from a friend who said he's learned that Roger's been asking lots of questions about Phoenix Paints."

"What's he learned?" A cold chill scooted down Julia's back. Three years ago she'd literally handed Roger the formula for the latest advancement in house paints in over thirty years. A month before Conrad Industries' new line of paints was scheduled to hit the market, their plant burned to the ground. Within three weeks Roger had left the company and Ideal Paints was marketing Conrad Industries' new product.

Because of the fire, it was impossible to meet the demand for their innovation, while Ideal Paints was capable of delivering paint to every hardware store in the country.

"Double security around the plant," Julia suggested.

"I've already done that."

"Who has Roger contacted?" she asked, pushing the hair from her forehead. They couldn't allow him to steal from them again.

"I have no way of knowing." Jerry sounded equally concerned.

"Do you think we should bring in a private investigator?"

"For what?"

"Tracking phones calls. See if he's getting information from any of our employees? We could have him watched. What do you think?"

"The hell if I know what to think. This all sounds crazy. It's like a nightmare happening all over again. How soon did Alek say the new products would be ready for marketing?"

"Soon. He's been working a lot of hours lately."

"I think we should move ahead as quickly as possible, don't you? I'll see what I can do to schedule a meeting with the marketing folks. The sooner we can get the product out on the store shelves, the better."

"Okay. Let me know if you hear anything," Julia requested.

"I will," Jerry promised.

They said a few words of farewell and when she replaced the telephone receiver, she sighed.

"What was that all about?" Alek asked.

Julia shook her head, not wanting to explain, because explaining would invariably involve telling him about her relationship with Roger. That was something she wanted to avoid.

"These lines," he said, tracing his finger along the creases in her brow, "are because of Roger Stanhope, aren't they, my love?"

Julia nodded.

"That is what I thought. Tell me about him, Julia. It's time I knew."

Chapter Nine

"Julia." Alek pressed her when she didn't immediately respond.

"Roger was just a man I once knew and trusted... several years ago. He proved he wasn't trustworthy. Can we leave it at that?"

"You loved him?"

Admitting it hurt her pride. Mixed in with all the regrets and the guilt was the shame. Her only crime had been loving a man who didn't deserve her devotion. A man who used her, and shocked her with his betrayal, so much so she refused to believe he was responsible until her father had literally shoved the evidence at her. Even then she'd made excuses for him, unable to accept the truth. Her father had become so exasperated with her that he'd... Julia turned her thoughts from that fateful day when her life had turned into a living nightmare.

"Yes, I loved him," she answered finally. "It was a mistake. A very bad one."

"What was your mistake?" Alek probed gently.

"It's too involved. I learned my lesson."

"And what was that?"

"That...love sometimes hurts."

Alek studied her for several moments, but what he was hoping to read, Julia could only speculate.

"Love doesn't always bring pain," he said, his gaze tender. "My love will prove otherwise." He kissed her with a compassion that brought tears to her eyes. She managed to blink them back and offer him a look of gratitude.

"Come," he said softly, lifting her into his arms. "It's time for bed."

"But..." Twisting around, she pointed to the carpet next to the fireplace where they'd made love only a half hour earlier. He couldn't possibly mean what she thought he meant. When she turned to look at him, she noticed a devilish glint in his eyes.

"Aleksandr!"

"My love," he said, nibbling on the side of her neck, "I warned you I'm a hungry man. This is your penance for keeping me frustrated all these weeks."

Julia threw back her head and laughed. "You didn't tell me you were Superman."

"Who?"

"Never mind," she said, directing his mouth to hers.

At dawn Alek was suddenly awake. Moonlight waltzed across the bedroom walls and the room was still and silent. He could find no reason why he should be so alert so abruptly.

A chime rang the hour from the anniversary clock Julia kept on top of her television. It was an hour before dawn and by all that was right, he should be exhausted. He was drained, sated and happy. His wife slept contentedly at his side, her slim body curled against his own. He kissed her cheek, grateful for the special woman she was. She'd led him on the chase of his life, the pursuit had been exhausting, but the prize was of the highest value.

He'd wanted to ask her more about Stanhope, but he could see the raw anguish the man's name brought to her eyes and even his curiosity wasn't worth causing her additional pain.

Alek knew little of this man, but what he did know, he didn't like. He'd seen the way Roger had reached for Julia, placing his hand on her arm as though he had a right to touch her, to make demands on her. Alek didn't like the way the other man had looked at Julia, either, with a leer, as if he could have her for his own with only a few persuasive words.

Alek hadn't thought of himself as a jealous man, but the quiet rage that roared through him when he found Roger Stanhope pestering Julia couldn't be denied.

The man was weak. One look told Alek as much. Stanhope relied on his sleek good looks, his flashy smile and compelling personality instead of intelligence, honest work and business acumen.

Alek wasn't fooled. Roger Stanhope was a worthy opponent. One that deeply concerned not only Julia, but Jerry, as well. Julia hadn't explained the telephone conversation she'd had with her brother, even when he'd asked.

Although she'd tried to make light of Jerry's call, Alek had caught snatches of the conversation, enough to know that she was worried. She'd been unable to disguise her distress. Stanhope wasn't worth causing Julia one iota of anxiety. As her husband, it was up to him to make sure the man who had betrayed her and her family wouldn't be allowed to do so again.

Alek was gone when Julia woke and she instantly experienced a surge of disappointment. One look at the clock explained Alek's absence. The last time she'd slept past ten o'clock had been as a teenager.

Nevertheless, she missed him. A slow, satisfied smile spread over her lips. She'd married quite a man. Apparently he worked with as much energy and enthusiasm as he made love.

She climbed out of bed and dressed casually. Since it was Saturday, and her week had been hellish, she intended to relax. There would be plenty of problems for her to deal with Monday morning. The desire to rush into her office was nil. Monday would be soon enough.

She was knotting the belt on her pink silk robe when she wandered into the kitchen. Anna was there, busily whipping up a bowl of something delicious, no doubt.

"Good morning, Anna."

"Good morning." Alek's sister stopped what she was doing and brought Julia a cup of coffee.

Being waited on was a luxury that would soon spoil Julia. "I'll take care of myself," she told her, not unkindly. "You go back to what you're doing." She wandered over to the counter and on closer examination the contents of Anna's efforts resembled cookie dough. A sample confirmed her suspicion. Oatmeal raisin, by her best guess.

"Yum."

Anna grinned at the compliment. "Alek asked me to bake them this morning for your picnic."

Julia paused halfway across the kitchen floor. "Our picnic?"

"Yes, he left me a note asking me to pack a basket of food. He gave me a long list of everything he wanted. I don't think he plans to return soon."

"Where is he?" Julia asked, adding a teaspoon of milk into her coffee. "Do you know?"

Anna shook her head as she resumed stirring the thick batter. "No. He had some errand, I think. He doesn't tell me much, I'm only his sister."

"He doesn't tell me much, either," Julia added with a short laugh. "I'm only his wife."

Anna giggled. "He should be back soon. He said you were very tired and wanted to be sure you slept as long as you needed. I'm very sorry to hear about your grandmother."

"Thank you—I'm sorry, too," Julia said, breathing in deeply at the fresh stab of pain she experienced at the mention of Ruth's passing. The hurt would be with her for a long while, she realized. Losing her grandmother had left a wide, gaping hole in her heart. Alek's love had gone a long way toward the healing process, but she would always miss Ruth.

Sitting down at the table with the morning paper, Julia tried to focus her attention on the headlines that were printed across the front page. Soon the words blurred and ran together. The tears came as an unwelcome surprise.

She brushed them from her cheeks, embarrassed by the display of emotion. She didn't dare look up for fear Anna would notice, and Julia wanted to hide how emotional she remained over her grandmother.

The sound of the front door opening announced Alek's return. Julia hurriedly wiped the moisture from her cheeks and smiled up at him. She hadn't fooled him, she realized, but it didn't matter as he strolled over to her, his eyes full of love, and kissed her soundly.

Julia had trouble not losing herself in his kiss. It would have been so easy to let their simple exchange lead to something more, and they both knew it.

Alek glanced impatiently over his shoulder toward his sister. "I'll give her the rest of the day off," he whispered.

"Don't be silly."

The hunger in his eyes convinced her how very serious he was. He lifted her effortlessly from her chair, sat down and tucked her in his lap.

"You slept late?" he questioned, smoothing the hair away from her face.

"Very late. You should have gotten me up."

"I was tempted. Tomorrow I will have no qualms about waking you as a husband should."

"Really?" she asked, loving him so much it felt as if her heart would burst wide open. She saw Anna watching them and it seemed Alek's sister was pleased at the closeness the two had found. "We're going on a picnic?"

"Yes," Alek said, his face brightening like that of a boy.

"Where?"

"That's my surprise. Pack a sweater, an extra set of clothes and a..." He hesitated, as if searching for a word, something he rarely did. His eyes widened. "A kite."

"Kite... as in flying-in-the-wind kite?"

He nodded enthusiastically.

Julia went still. "Alek," she said, studying him, "Are you taking me to the ocean?"

"Yes, my love, the ocean."

Within fifteen minutes they were on their way. Anna's basket of goodies was tucked away in the back seat, along with an extra set of clothes for them both, several beach towels, a blanket and no less than five different varieties of kites.

Alek drove to Ocean Shores. The sun was out and the surf pounded against the sandy shore with a roar that echoed toward them. The scent of salt stung the air. Sea gulls soared overhead, looking for an opportune meal. There were plenty of people, but nothing like the crowded beaches along the Oregon and California coasts.

Alek parked the car and found them an ideal spot to spread out their blanket and bask in the sunshine. Julia removed her shoes and ran barefoot in the warm sand after him.

"This is perfect," she cried, throwing her arms out and circling around several times. "I love it."

Alek returned to the car for their picnic basket and the kites and joined her on the blanket. He looked more relaxed than she could ever remember seeing him. He plopped down beside her and stretched out as if he'd been tied down.

The wind buffeted against them and then Alek moved, positioning himself behind her. He wrapped his arms around her and inhaled slowly, drawing the salty, clean air into his lungs. Julia followed suit, breathing in the clean fresh scent of the sea.

"It's so peaceful here," Julia commented. There were a large number of activities around them, including horseback riding, kite flying, a football-throwing contest, even a couple of volleyball games, but none of those distracted from the serenity she experienced.

"I thought you'd feel this way." He kissed the side of her neck.

Julia relaxed against his strength, letting him absorb her weight.

"My mother often brought Anna and me to the Baltic Sea after our father was killed."

Julia knew shockingly little about her husband's life before he came to the United States. "How old were you when he died?"

"Ten. Anna was seven."

"How did he die?"

It seemed an eternity passed before Alek spoke, and when he did his voice was dark and low. "He was murdered. I don't think we will ever know the real reasons why. They came, the soldiers, in the middle of the night. We were all asleep. I woke to my mother's screams but by the time I got past the soldier guarding the door, my father had already been killed."

"Oh, Alek." Julia's throat tightened with the effort to hold back the tears.

"We learned from someone who risked his life to tell us that the KGB suspected my father of illegal activities, but that made no sense to us since my father was a chemist and a loyal Communist. His explanation raised more questions than it answered.''

''If your government suspected your father was doing something illegal, then why not try him before a court and give him a chance to defend himself? What they did was barbaric.''

''Yes,'' he agreed, ''and it nearly destroyed my mother. If it had not been for Anna and me, I believe my mother would have died, too. Not from the soldiers' hands, although I have no doubt they would shoot a woman, not when they didn't hesitate to gun down a defenseless man, but from grief.''

''What happened afterward?''

''My mother had to support us. Both Anna and I did everything we could to help, but it was difficult. Because I was a good student, I was given the opportunity to study at the university. It was there that I met my first American. I couldn't believe the freedom the students told me about. I've always been good with languages—Anna, too. Soon afterward, I started learning English. After I met Jerry, he sent me many books in your language. He was my one link to America.''

''Were you surprised when he asked you to come work for Conrad Industries?''

''Yes.''

''Did Jerry ever tell you about his beautiful younger sister?'' Julia prodded.

''In passing.''

''Were you curious about me?''

''No,'' Alek answered without hesitation.

She poked him in the ribs with the sharp point of her elbow and was rewarded with a mock cry of pain from him.

"I'll be more curious now," he promised.

"Good."

His hand edged its way beneath her blouse.

"Alek!"

"I'm just wondering how fast I can make you want me."

"Fast enough. Now stop, we're on a public beach."

He sighed as though her words had wounded him deeply. "Maybe we should rent a hotel room."

"We could have done that in Seattle. Since we're at the beach and the day is gorgeous, let's enjoy ourselves."

"Julia," Alek said sternly, "trust me, we would enjoy ourselves in a hotel room, too."

Smiling, she leaned back her head to look at him. "No one bothered to tell me you were just a sex fiend."

"This is a surprise to me, too. You do this to me, Julia, only you." He moved against her and she felt the tightness in his jeans against her backside.

"I promise I'll satisfy your carnal appetite," she assured him. "And I'm a woman of my word."

"I must stop being so selfish," Alek said, suddenly serious. The teasing quality was gone from his voice. "I didn't bring you here to make love, I brought you here to heal. After my father was killed, my mother made weekly trips to the ocean with Anna and me. It was a time of solace for us, sitting on the beach. The ocean went a long way toward healing us. I hoped it would help you, too."

"It does," Julia said, looking out at the pounding surf.

"You must forgive my greed for you."

"Only if you forgive my greed for you." The love-making was so new between them, they were eager to learn everything they could about each other, eager to give and eager to receive. Julia didn't fool herself into believing this kind of desire would continue. If it did, they were both slated to die of sheer exhaustion.

"I want you to relax in my arms," Alek instructed, "and close you eyes." He waited a moment. "Are they closed?"

She nodded. The sounds that came at her were incredible. The ocean as it slapped against the shore, the cry of the birds and the roar of the scooters as they shot past her, kicking up the sand. The smells, carried on the wind, were pungent.

"Now open your eyes."

Julia obeyed and was swamped with the richness of color. The sky was blue with huge marshmallow clouds that banked the horizon. The water was a murky green that left a thin, white, frothy trail. Every color was vibrant and detailed. Julia's breath caught in her throat at the beauty that spread before her.

"Oh, Alek, it's so lovely."

"My mother did that with Anna and me, but I think she was doing it for herself, too, so we could see that life could be good, if we looked around at the world instead of within ourselves."

That was what Julia had been doing these past few years, looking at the darkness and the shortcomings within herself. Under a microscope, her faults had seemed glaring. It was little wonder that she'd been so miserable.

"Alek," she said, nearly overwhelmed with her discovery, "thank you, thank you so much."

They kissed and it was as if his love was an absolution for all that had gone before and all that would come later. She twisted around and looped her arms around his neck and held him. Tears rained down her face, but these were tears of release, tears of vindication for herself.

Alek knew his relationship with Julia changed that afternoon at the ocean. In some small, imperceptible way, matters were different between them. More open, more trusting.

That evening, the day after their venture to the beach, Alek needed to run down to the laboratory. When he told Julia, she offered to ride with him, as if even an hour apart was more than she could bear.

Her willingness had taken him by surprise.

"You're sure?" he asked.

"Of course. It'll do me good to get out of the house."

They listened to a classical music station on the way across town. Security had tightened at the laboratory, Alek noted, but he didn't give it more than a passing thought. Julia went with him into the office. He found what he needed and brought it back to the apartment.

"Would you like some coffee?"

"Please." Her willingness to see to his small pleasure was something of a surprise, too, a pleasant one at that.

While he read over the latest report, Julia was content to sit at his side, absorbed in a novel. He couldn't remember a time when she'd voluntarily sat still. Her body had always seemed to be filled with nervous energy, as if there were people to see, places to go. That was gone from her now and in its place had come a restfulness.

"I'm not anxious to return to work in the morning," she said when Alek was done reading the report. Leaning against him, she stretched her legs out along the sofa and heaved a giant sigh. "These past few days have been so wonderful. I don't know if I'm ready to deal with the real world again."

"Will you always work, Julia?"

"I . . . don't know. I hadn't thought about it. I suppose I will until after the children are born at any rate, but even then I'll still be involved in the management of the company."

"Then you wouldn't mind if we had a family."

"No, of course I wouldn't mind. Did you think I would?"

"I wasn't sure."

"Then rest assured, my Russian lover, I would welcome your children."

Alek felt his heart expand with eagerness. Unfortunately it wasn't the only thing expanding. "So you'd like a family," he said tentatively. "Would you mind if we worked on this project soon?"

"How soon?" she asked, eyeing him skeptically.

His hands fiddled with the buttons of her top. "Now," he said, aware of the husky sound of his voice.

Julia sighed that womanly sigh he'd come to recognize as a signal of her eagerness for him. "I think we might be able to arrange something."

"Julia, my love," Alek said with a groan, "I fear I'll never get enough of you. What have you done to me? Are you a witch who's cast some spell over me?"

Julia laughed. "If anyone has cast a spell over anyone, it's you over me. I find myself lonely without you. If we can't be together, I feel lost and empty. I never thought I could love again, and you've shown me the way."

Alek gave a deep, throaty laugh and placed his hands under her breasts, weighing their heaviness in his palms. Slowly, deliberately, she leaned back, arching upward so the peaks of her breasts were presented to him.

"Julia." He rasped her name and, folding her over his arm, bent forward to cover her soft reaching mouth with his. The kiss revealed their need for each other. He heard Julia's novel fall off the sofa and hit the floor, but neither cared. His hands were busy with her front and once her shirt was open, she twisted around.

"I vote for the bed this time."

"The bed," he said mockingly. "Where's your sense of adventure?"

Julia laughed softly and teased him unmercifully with the tip of her tongue. "It was used up in the bathtub this morning. I'll have you know it took me twenty minutes to clean the water off the floor."

He carried her into their bedroom, deposited her onto the mattress, all the while kissing her. Julia barely had time to remove her jeans before he entered her warm, passionate body. Alek would have felt guilty at his eagerness to make love to her, if she hadn't revealed the same level of anticipation.

Once he was buried to the hilt inside her hot, throbbing moistness, he sighed and bent down to kiss her.

"I didn't know anything felt this good," she told him, looping her arms around his neck and lifting her torso so her bare breasts seared his chest.

Alek didn't know, either. Nothing had ever been this good in his life.

Afterward, they lay on the bed. Julia was sprawled across him. Every now and again she kissed him, or he kissed her. Alek had never known such contentment in his life. It frightened him. Happiness had always been fleeting, and he wasn't sure he could trust what he'd found with Julia. His hold on her tightened and he closed his eyes and discovered he couldn't imagine what his life would be without her now. Bleak and empty, he decided.

When Jerry had first suggested marriage, Alek had set his terms. He wasn't a believer in love. It seemed love came at the expense of everything else. Alek couldn't very well claim he'd never been in love before. There'd been a handful of relationships over the years. He'd fancied himself in love a couple of times, but he'd always grown bored and restless after a short while. He was a disappointment to his mother, who was looking for him and Anna to supply her with a houseful of grandchildren to spoil.

How perceptive his sister was to realize he hadn't loved Julia in the beginning. He hadn't expected to ever love her. He offered her his loyalty and his devotion, but had held his heart in reserve. She had it now, though, in her palm. His heart, indeed his very life.

Julia lay across her husband's body and sighed deeply, utterly and completely content. She'd never known a time like this with a man. A time of peace and discovery. His talk of children had unleashed a truck-load of long-buried dreams.

They hadn't bothered to use protection. Not even once. They each seemed to pretend it didn't matter, what would be would be.

Pregnant.

She rolled the word through her mind as though it were foreign to her, and in many ways it was. Even two weeks ago she would have sworn it was impossible. Now, thoughts of a family filled her mind and her heart. Perhaps it was because she'd so recently lost Ruth and that one of the last things her grandmother had said to her referred to the children that were waiting to be born.

After so many years of pain, Julia hardly knew how to deal with happiness. In some ways she was afraid to trust that it would last. She'd been happy with Roger and then everything had blown up in her face. The crushing pain of his deception would never leave her. She'd lost the desire to punish him. Conrad Industries' runaway success would be revenge enough. He wasn't likely to be hired by any other company outside of Ideal Paints. After what had happened, no one else would trust him. Without realizing what he was doing, he'd painted himself in a corner. She smiled at her own sorry pun.

"Something amuses you?" Alek asked, apparently having felt her smile.

"Yes . . . and no."

"That sounds rather vague to me."

"Rest," she urged.

"Why?" he challenged. "Do you have something physical in mind?"

Julia grinned once more. "If I don't, I'm sure you do. Now hush, I'm trying to sleep."

"Then I suggest you stop making those little hip movements."

Julia hadn't been conscious she was moving. "Sorry."

He clamped his hands over her buttocks. "Don't be, I'm not."

Julia closed her eyes and returned to her daydream. A baby would turn her world upside down. She'd never been very domestic. If her child-rearing skills were on the level of her cooking skills, then she...

"Now you're frowning." Alek chastised her. "What's wrong?"

"I ... I was just thinking I might not be a very good mother. I hardly know anything about babies. I might really botch this children thing."

He captured her head and brought her mouth to his to silence her with a kiss. "You're going to be a wonderful mother. We'll learn about all this together when the time arrives. Agreed?"

Julia emptied her lungs of air. "You're right. As a business person I know it, but as a woman, I'm not so sure."

"Listen, woman, you're making it damned impossible to nap. As far as I can make out, there's only one way to keep you quiet." With his arms gripping her waist, he transferred her onto her back and nuzzled her neck until Julia cried out and promised to do as he said.

Monday morning, Julia arrived at the office bright and early. Virginia, her secretary, showed up a few minutes after she did, looking flustered and unsure.

"I'm sorry, I didn't realize you were planning to be here quite so early. If I had, I would have come in before eight myself. I'll get your coffee right away."

"Don't worry about it," Julia said, reaching for the stack of mail in her in-basket. Her desk was neatly organized, and she was grateful Virginia had taken the time to lighten her load.

"I read over the mail and answered everything I could," Virginia said hesitatingly. "I hope you don't mind."

"Of course not. I'm grateful for your help."

Virginia looked mildly surprised and hurried out of the office, returning a few minutes later with a steaming cup of coffee. "I'm sorry but there doesn't seem to be any cream. I'll send out for some right away."

"I can live without cream," Julia said absently, reaching for the stack of phone messages of which there were no less than thirty. "Would you ask my brother to stop in when it's convenient and contact my husband and see if he could meet me for lunch?" She stopped, realizing for the first time that she probably already had a luncheon appointment. "That is, if I'm not already tied up."

"You were scheduled to meet with Mr. Casey, but I wasn't sure if you'd feel up to dealing with him your first day back. I took the liberty of scheduling the luncheon for Tuesday."

Virginia knew Doug Casey was one of her least favorite people and she smiled her appreciation. "Great, thanks."

"I'll get back to you in just a minute," Virginia said. True to her word, her secretary returned no more than a few minutes later. "Your brother will be down shortly and your husband suggests you meet at noon at the Freeway Park."

"Great." She returned to the matters at hand and didn't hear Virginia leave her office.

Jerry strolled inside her office looking anything but casual. "I'm worried about Stanhope. I think he's up to something. I've got a private investigator following him. If he makes contact with any of our people, we'll know about it."

Julia rolled a pen between her palms. "I can't believe any of our employees would sell us out, do you?"

Jerry tensed and shrugged. "After what happened last time, who's to tell?"

"Let me know if you hear anything."

"I will. The investigator is going to make regular reports."

Her brother left shortly thereafter and Julia was dealing with a large stack of correspondence when she noted the time. She stopped in the middle of a dictation.

Virginia raised her head, anticipating Julia's next move.

"We'll continue this after lunch," she said, standing and reaching for her purse. "I probably won't be back until after one. Cover for me if need be."

"Of course." Virginia was on her feet, too, and Julia felt her secretary's scrutiny. Thinking there might be something wrong with her, she twisted around to be sure her slip wasn't showing.

"Is something wrong?" she asked the older woman.

"No," Virginia said with a shy smile. "Something's very right.

"Oh?" Julia didn't understand.

"I don't think I've ever seen you look happier."

Chapter Ten

Freeway Park was one of Seattle's more innovative ideas. A large grassy area built over the top of a freeway. Green ivy spilled over the concrete banks, reaching their spindly arms toward the roadway far below.

At noontime many of the Seattle office workers converged on the area to enjoy their lunches in the opulent sunshine. Each summer the city offered a series of free concerts at regular intervals. Julia didn't know if there was one scheduled for that afternoon, but nothing could have made her day more perfect than to meet her husband.

She saw Alek from across the lush green grass and started toward him. It seemed he saw her at the same time because he grinned broadly and stepped her way, as well.

"Did you bring anything for your lunch?" he asked, after they kissed briefly.

Eating was something Julia often failed to think about. "Ah, no, I forgot."

"I thought as much. Luckily you have a husband who knows his wife. Come, let's find a place to sit down."

"What'd you buy?" she asked, noting the white sack in his hand.

"Fish and chips. Do you approve?"

"Sounds great." She was hungry she realized, something that was a rarity. Generally she ate because it was necessary to live, but not for any real enjoyment. Anna was sure to change that. Alek's sister cooked tempting breakfasts and left delicious three- and four-course dinners ready to be served when they arrived home. By the end of the year, Julia predicted she'd be fat and... pregnant. The thought produced a deep inner excitement.

Alek found a spot for them on a park bench. He set the white bag between them and lifted out an order of fish-and-chips packed in a thick cardboard container.

"Are you trying to fatten me up?" she teased.

His eyes fairly twinkled. "Already you know me so well."

"Indeed I do," she teased.

"But the question is," Alek said, eyeing her speculatively, "do you like me?"

It was a task to pull her gaze away from his magnetic eyes. "More each day," she answered, her voice dipping slightly with sincerity.

An electric moment passed before Alek spoke. "You won't be working late tonight, will you?"

"No. Will you?"

He shook his head. "I plan to be home at five-fifteen."

"That early?" She generally didn't leave the office until after six.

"I'll be lucky to last that long," he whispered, and the hungry look in his eyes had nothing to do with the order of fish-and-chips in his hand.

There was no missing his meaning. Julia's body went into a state of overdrive. She'd never thought of herself as a highly sexual person, but in that instant she knew she had to do something to appease the overwhelming urge she had to make love to her husband.

"Alek . . . would you mind kissing me?"

He blinked, then bent his head, meaning only to brush her lips she was sure, but that wouldn't be near enough to satisfy her. Not any longer. She slipped her tongue forward, teasing and taunting him.

A low moan came from deep within his throat, which aroused her as nothing ever had before. The kiss deepened and deepened until they were lost in each other.

She wrenched her mouth from his, gasping with need and with lack of oxygen. "Five-fifteen," she said when she could manage to speak.

"I'll be there waiting."

Jerry was lingering in her office when Julia returned from lunch. He was pacing like a caged animal. Without greeting her or any form of prologue, he announced, "Roger's made contact with someone from the laboratory."

Julia was stunned into speechlessness. "How do you know?" she asked when she could. A cold, sinking sensation attacked her stomach. Deep-fried fish aided the sickening feeling.

"Rich Peck."

"Who the hell is Rich Peck?"

Jerry spun around and glared at her as if she were illiterate. "The private eye I hired. Rich managed to trace the telephone numbers that came into Roger's home for the past several days."

"How did he do something like that?"

"Julia," Jerry said, clearly exasperated with her, "that isn't what's important just now. What is important is that someone from Conrad Industries contacted Roger. They used the phone from the laboratory."

"But who?"

"That's the point. It could have been any number of people. The phone's used by nearly all the staff. What I'm saying is that we've got a traitor on our hands."

Julia found that hard to believe. Most everyone who was employed at the laboratory had been with them three years earlier. Their dislike of Roger was well-known. After the fire it had taken several months to rebuild the company. Julia had tried to keep as many employees on the payroll as possible during that lag time, in order not to lose her trained and most loyal help. There were twenty or more who'd been with Conrad Industries fifteen years or better. The strain on the budget to pay employees crippled the company financially. Nearly every employee had gone two months on the promise of reimbursement once Julia could get the company back on its feet.

In retrospect the promise of reimbursement may not have seemed like much, but Julia appreciated their sacrifice. And their trust. Her father had recently died, and to say she was green behind the ears would have been a gross understatement. The company was on the verge of bankruptcy. It was one of the bleakest times in Julia's life and in the company's history.

Ruth's amazing faith in her to pull the company out of its financial nosedive was what helped Julia survive those grim times.

To discover that someone working in the laboratory was selling her out now seemed impossible. She refused to believe it. Refused to accept it.

"What do you think we should do?" Jerry asked.

Julia walked over to the window and stared down at the street ten floors below. The miniature-size cars and people seemed to be moving in slow motion. It was as if she was staring at another world that wasn't linked to her own.

"Nothing," she said after a thought-filled moment. "We do nothing."

"But..."

"What can we do?" she demanded impatiently. "All we have is the knowledge that someone contacted Roger. Should we haul every employee in for questioning by Peck, hoping his expertise at grilling fifty-year-old men and women will flush out whoever wants to betray us?"

"We could have Alek scout around and..."

"No," she said quickly, interrupting him. "Alek is as much a suspect as anyone else."

"Don't be ridiculous. Alek's got more reason than anyone to make sure Phoenix Paints succeeds. It's his baby. He's poured his life's blood into this project. Surely you don't think he'd betray us."

"No, I don't," she agreed readily enough. "But that doesn't change the facts. Roger had every reason for Conrad Industries to prosper, too, and look what happened."

"But Alek . . ."

"Alek is a suspect. I warn you, Jerry, don't say a word of this to him. Not one single word."

Her brother stared at her as if she were mad. "He's your husband. My God, you don't even trust your own husband."

"You're right," she admitted, "I don't. You can thank Roger for that. I wouldn't trust my own mother after the lesson Roger taught me. If you think I'm a coldhearted bitch, then fine. I'd rather have you think poorly of me than hand over the fate of this company to a man who can destroy us."

Making love to his wife was probably the most fabulous sensation Alek had ever experienced. Perhaps it was because she'd withheld herself from him so long that he treasured the prize so highly. Julia was open, honest and genuine.

Alek had never lost control of himself with another woman, but he had with Julia. She was fast becoming as necessary as the air he breathed. He wanted her, and that need was growing at an alarming rate. He'd make love to her and then instantly wonder how long it would be before he could have her again.

Julia was incredible because each time they were intimate, she gave him a little more of herself. A little more of her trust. A little more of her heart. A little more of her soul.

He glanced at his watch and frowned. It was well past the time they'd agreed to meet. Knowing Julia, she'd probably got caught up in her work and let time slip away from her.

He waited another ten minutes before reaching for the phone and dialing her office number. Her secretary answered.

"This is Alek. Has Julia left the office yet?"

"No." Virginia sounded surprised. "She's still here. Would you like me to connect you?"

"Please." He waited a moment before Julia came on the line.

"Hello," she said absently. Alek could picture her sitting behind her desk with her reading glasses propped at the end of her sweet, upturned nose. No doubt she was embroiled in some hopelessly tangled project.

"Do you know what time it is?"

"Five-forty. Why?"

"We had an appointment, remember? I've got a deck of cards with me and . . ."

"A deck of cards?"

He wasn't sure what it was he heard in her voice, but it wasn't amusement. It troubled him, but he didn't have time to analyze it just then. "Yes, I recently heard about this card game that originated in America that I want to play with you."

"A card game?"

"Strip poker. Sounds like a fun game to me. I've got everything ready and waiting. How much longer are you going to be?"

"Oh, Alek, listen, I'm really sorry, but I could be here another hour or more. Everything's piled up on my desk from last week. I really shouldn't leave."

"I understand." He didn't like it, but he understood. "My game can wait, and it looks like I'll have to, too." He was hoping for a little sympathy, or at least a shred of regret, but he received neither.

Something was wrong. Alek could feel it in his blood. Julia was keeping something from him. He read it in her voice, felt it as clearly as if it were a tangible thing.

Julia didn't arrive home until nearly nine. It would be too much to ask that Alek not be there waiting for her. She didn't know how she was going to look him in the eye.

A headache had been building from the moment Jerry had left her office. Everything in her told her that Alek would be the last person who'd sell her out. It would make it much easier to believe in him if she hadn't so staunchly defended Roger to her father. She'd been wrong once and the price had nearly demanded her sanity.

Alek greeted her at the door. Without a word he drew her into his arms and hugged her. She was swallowed in his embrace, surrounded by his love, and she soaked it up, needing it so badly.

"Tell me what's troubling you?" he asked.

How he knew was beyond her. She had no choice but to sidestep the question. "What makes you think anything is wrong?"

"I'm your husband. I know you."

"I've got a terrible headache."

He studied her as if he wasn't sure he should believe her, although it was true enough. Her temples throbbed and she was exhausted. "Did you eat dinner?" she asked, wanting to turn the subject away from herself.

"No, I wanted to wait for you. Are you ready?"

Her appetite was nil. "I'm not very hungry. If you don't mind, I'd like to soak in the bath." She left him without waiting for his response.

The hot water was soothing and a full thirty minutes passed before she could bring herself to leave the comfort. She dressed for bed, mentally and physically exhausted. Alek was waiting for her when she finished. He seemed to anticipate her every need, which increased her feelings of guilt.

He followed her into the bedroom. "Would you like me to rub your temples?" he asked, sitting on the edge of the mattress and staring down on her.

"You'd do that?"

He seemed surprised by her question. "Of course. You are my love, the very blood that flows through my veins. There is nothing I wouldn't do for you."

"Oh, Alek," she moaned.

"This is strange. American husbands do not love their wives this way?"

"I . . . I don't know, I've never been married before, but my guess is that no, husbands don't generally offer to do such things for their wives."

"Come," he said, sitting on their bed, bracing his back against the headboard, and stretching out his long legs. "Rest your head on my thigh and I'll soothe away your pain. Would you like me to sing to you again?" He reached for the light at the side of the bed and twisted the switch.

"Please." The meaning of what he was singing was beyond her, but she loved the deep, melodic sound of his voice. As he sang, his nimble fingers gently soothed away the throbbing pain in her head. She was sleepy when he finished. Gently lifting her head from his lap, he began to leave her. It was then that Julia realized how much she wanted him to stay.

"Don't leave," she pleaded softly. "Come to bed with me."

He whispered something in Russian and it sounded as if he felt she was asking for the impossible.

"For a few minutes," he agreed with obvious reluctance. He undressed in the dark and slipped beneath the sheets. He gathered her in his arms and their arms and legs tangled.

Julia lifted her mouth to his and his lips were hot on hers. His hand eased upward to cup her breast. Her hand found its own quest and her eyes widened with wonder at the rigid strength of him.

Alek gasped at the intimate contact and when Julia looked at him she noted that his face was twisted as he fought for control.

"I should leave," he said, sounding breathless. He also sounded as if he very much wanted to stay.

"No," she said.

"Julia, you don't understand, a man..."

She stroked the throbbing heat of his erection. "I understand very well, trust me." As she spoke she was moving over him, bracing one knee on each side of him.

Alek arched upward instinctively. "Julia...for the love of heaven."

"You eased my ache, now I'll ease yours." She parted her thighs and settled over him, swallowing his heat, taking him fully into her. Completely. Alek's breath dissolved into deep shudders.

Her own breath vanished. Soon it was replaced with harmonizing long, low moans as they found their release in each other.

Alek held her a long time afterward and she savored these moments of closeness as the warm magic of his love stole over her. Alek filled all the empty spaces in her life. He soothed away the feelings of abandonment and loss. He loved her as no man ever had. He was gentle and giving.

Just before she entered the welcome folds of slumber, she heard Alek whisper something about hoping she suffered from a bad headache again very soon.

Julia was restless. She didn't understand why she couldn't manage to sit still. Then again, she could. It was only natural to be nervous given the phone call she'd received earlier that morning. It had been a week since Jerry had hired Rich Peck and he'd phoned wanting to give her his first weekly report. Since Jerry was out for the afternoon, Julia had agreed to meet with the private investigator herself.

Virginia announced his arrival and Peck entered her office. He was tall and wiry, and much younger than she'd anticipated. Perhaps thirty, if that.

"Hello," he said, stepping forward and shaking her hand.

"Please sit down," Julia invited.

He took the chair on the other side of her desk. "This Stanhope fellow is an interesting character," he began. "I've been tailing him for nearly a week now. I managed to catch snapshots of just about everyone he's met. My guess is that whoever is leaking information to him is a woman. Once you get a look at the photographs you'll understand why. He's quite the ladies' man.''

This wasn't news to Julia, who'd been Roger's victim herself.

Rich brought out a folder thick with photographs, reached for a small pad, the type reporters use, and flipped through the first couple of pages.

"He had several business lunches, as best as I can tell. Although we've got a twenty-four-hour tail on him, there are certain periods of time we can't account for.''

"I see. Do you think he knows he's being followed?''

Rich snickered lightly. ''The guy hasn't got a clue. He's not the real intelligent type, if you know what I mean. He lives on the edge, too. I talked with his landlady and learned he was two months behind on his rent. It's happened before. His credit rating's so full of holes he couldn't get a loan if his life depended on it.''

"What about his position with Ideal Paints? Is that secure?''

"Who knows? From what I've been able to learn, he doesn't have many friends. He seems to get along all right on the job. As for what he does with his money, that isn't hard to figure out. The guy goes out on the town every night with a different woman. He seems to get his kicks showing off to others what a stud he is.''

This too didn't come as any surprise to Julia. Roger liked to refer to himself as a party animal.

"Go ahead and look through those photographs and see if there's anyone you recognize. Take your time to be sure. I've got them stacked according to the day of the week. Thursday of this week is on the top. He left his apartment about ten. He seemed to be in something of a hurry and arrived at his office around ten-fifteen. He didn't leave again until four, and then came out a side entrance. My tail noted that some girl came out the front of the office building directly afterward and seemed to be looking for someone. Our best guess was that he was escaping her.

"He waited around ten or fifteen minutes and then left. He went home, changed his clothes and was out again by six. He picked up some chick and they went to dinner. He spent the night with her."

That too was typical.

"Wednesday..." Rich continued as Julia flipped through the stack of photographs. "Again he was late into the office. He arrived about ten and left again at eleven-thirty. He drove to Henshaw's, that fancy restaurant on Lake Union."

Julia nodded; she knew it well. An eternity earlier it had been one of their favorite places. The food was delicious and the ambience luxurious, but not overpowering.

"Whoever he was supposed to meet was waiting for him outside. My guess was this was a business lunch. The guy he was meeting was angry about something. The two of them had an exchange of words outside the restaurant. We got several excellent photos. It looked for a moment like they were going to have a fistfight. Frankly, Stanhope was smart to avoid this one. The guy would have pulverized him in seconds."

Julia flipped to the next series of snapshots. Her gaze fell upon Alek's angry face and she gasped.

Rich's attention reverted from the tablet to her. "You recognize him?"

Julia felt as if she was going to vomit.

"Ms. Conrad?"

She nodded.

"An employee?"

Once again she nodded. "Yes," she managed. "An employee. You can leave the rest of the photographs here and I'll go through them later. You've done an excellent job, Mr. Peck." She stood and ushered him to her door. "Jerry will be in touch with you sometime later this afternoon. I believe you've solved our mystery."

"Always glad to be of service."

"Thank you again."

Julia collapsed against the door the instant it was closed. Her stomach twisted into a giant knot of pain. This couldn't be happening. This couldn't be real. She felt dreadfully sick to her stomach and not knowing what else to do, emptied her lunch into her wastepaper basket. She was kneeling on the floor, her trembling hands holding her hair away from her face, when Virginia walked into her office.

"Oh dear, are you all right?"

Julia closed her eyes and nodded.

"Let me help you," the kindly woman offered. With her hand under Julia's elbow, she helped her to her feet. "You need to lie down."

"Could...would you see if you could find my brother for me?"

"You don't want me to call your husband?"

"No," she said forcefully, "get Jerry. Have him come as soon as he can . . . tell him it's an emergency."

Her legs were unstable and she literally slumped into her chair. In the past several years Julia had received many valuable lessons from pain. Roger had been her first teacher, but his tactics paled when compared to Alek's. It would have been easier if Alek had aimed a gun at her heart and pulled the trigger.

Julia didn't know how long it took her brother to arrive. Twenty minutes, she guessed, perhaps longer. She should be sobbing hysterically, instead she found herself as calm and cool as if the man who was betraying her and her brother were barely more than an acquaintance.

Jerry rushed into her office, apparently having run at least part of the way, because his face was red and he was breathless.

"Virginia said it was an emergency."

"I ... I was being a bit dramatic."

"Not according to Virginia. She wanted to know if she should phone for an ambulance. You're a little pale, but you look fine to me."

"I'm not, and you won't be, either, once you get a look at these." She handed him the series of three photographs.

The botchy redness faded from Jerry's face and he paled as he studied Rich Peck's snapshots.

"Alek?" he breathed in disbelief.

"It appears so."

"There's got to be some explanation."

"I'm sure there is." There always was. Something that sounded logical and believable. She'd been through this before, and knew all there was to know about betrayals of trust. When she'd confronted Roger, he'd worn this hurt, disbelieving look of shock and dismay that she could possible suspect him of anything so underhanded. He'd angrily declared his innocence, told her it was all a misunderstanding that he'd be able to clear up within a matter of minutes, given the opportunity. Because she loved him so desperately and because she wanted to believe him so badly, she'd listened. In the end it all made sense to her and she'd defended him because she loved and trusted him. She loved and trusted Alek, too, but she'd been wrong before, so very wrong, and it had cost her and her family dearly.

"What are you going to do?" Jerry asked in a whisper. He hadn't recovered yet himself. He continued to stare at the photographs as though the pictures would announce the truth if he studied them long enough.

"I don't know," she said unevenly.

"You aren't going to fire him, are you?"

"I don't know yet."

"Julia, for the love of heaven, Alek's your husband."

"I don't know what I'm going to do," she repeated. "I just don't know."

Jerry rubbed a hand over his face and inhaled deeply. "We should confront him, give him the opportunity to explain. It's possible that he's got a very good reason for meeting Roger that has nothing to do with Phoenix Paints."

"Jerry, you were ten before you gave up believing in Santa Claus. Remember? There's only one reason Alek would contact Roger and we both know it."

"That doesn't make any sense. Alek has more reason for Phoenix Paints to succeed than anyone. His career hinges on the success of our new line of products. Why would he deliberately sabotage himself? He spent years researching these developments." His hands pleaded with her and his eyes demanded that she respond.

"If you're looking to me for answers, I don't have any. Why do any of us do the things we do? My guess is that he was looking for revenge."

"Revenge? Alek? Now I know there's something wrong. We've been good to Alek, good to his family, and he's been good to us. He doesn't have any score to settle with us."

"Dad was good to Roger, too, remember? He was the one who gave Roger his first job. He hired him directly out of college when Dad could have taken on someone with far more experience. If we're looking for reasons why Alek would never do this, we'd be pulling scales over our own eyes."

Jerry studied her for several minutes. "I'm going to talk to him."

Julia folded her arms around her middle and nodded.

"Do you want to come with me?"

"No! I couldn't bear it. Not again." She closed her eyes and the upper half of her body swayed with her pain. "I can't believe this is happening."

"I can't believe it's happening, either."

"Why is it I continually fall in love with the wrong kind of man? Why, Jerry? There must be something fundamentally wrong with me."

Jerry walked to her window and stared out. His shoulders moved up and down with a deep sigh. "We're overreacting."

"Maybe," Julia agreed. "But I have that ache in the pit of my stomach again. The last time it was there was when Dad forced me to face the truth about Roger."

"The least we can do is listen to his explanation."

Julia shook her head. "You listen, I . . . can't." She didn't want to be there when Alek gave his excuse. She'd let her brother handle this because she was incapable of dealing with it.

Jerry's gaze narrowed. "I've never seen you like this. It's been a long time since you've been so detached."

"Let me guess," she returned sarcastically. "Could it have been following my breakup with Roger?"

"This is different. You're married to Alek."

"It's a little more involved, a little more complicated than before, but it's not so different. Until . . . this is resolved it would be better if Alek didn't come into work. Tell him that for me."

"Julia . . ."

"Tell him, Jerry, because I can't. Please." Her voice cracked. "It's just until this matter is settled. Alek will understand."

"But you aren't going to listen to his explanation?"

"No. You listen to what he has to say, but don't argue his case with me. I tried that with Dad, remember? I was so certain Roger was an innocent victim of circumstances."

Her brother stood and closed his eyes. He looked older, as though he'd aged ten years right before her eyes. Julia understood. She felt old herself. And sick. Her stomach pitched and heaved again.

Jerry left and her stomach pitched once again. Automatically she reached for the wastepaper basket.

Julia left the office an hour later. She wasn't sure where she intended on going, but she knew she couldn't stay there any longer. She started walking with no real course in mind and wandered down to the Pike Place Market. People were bustling about and, not wanting to be around a crowd, she headed for the waterfront. Not the tourist areas, but much farther down where the large cruising vessels docked.

She walked for hours, trying to sort through her emotions, and eventually gave up. She was in too much pain to think clearly.

She didn't cry. Not once. She figured it was the body's protective device that numbed her spirit.

It was well past dark and the area of town that she roamed wasn't any place for a woman to be wandering alone. It was as if she almost welcomed an attack. Perhaps subconsciously, she did.

Before long she found herself on the same street as her condominium. The security man looked surprised to find her arriving so late. He greeted her warmly and held open the heavy glass door for her.

The elevator ride up to her high rise seemed to take an eternity, but it wasn't slow enough. Soon she'd face her husband.

She'd barely gotten her key into the lock before the door was wrenched open. Alek loomed above her like a bad dream.

Chapter Eleven

The signs were there with Alek, Julia realized, the same ones Roger had worn with such indignation. The hurt, angry look that she could believe such a terrible thing of him. As if she were the betrayer. As if she were the guilty one.

Roger had turned the tables on her, too, with such finesse she didn't realize what was happening. Julia studied her husband and believed with all her heart that he would never betray her.

"Where have you been?" Alek demanded next. "I've been worried sick."

"I went for a walk."

"For five hours?"

She moved past him. "I should have phoned. I'm sorry, but I needed to think."

Alek followed her. "Why didn't you come to me yourself? Instead you sent Jerry." His words spoke of his pain. "I don't deny talking to Roger Stanhope, but at least give me the chance to explain why."

"You can't very well deny seeing him since we have the evidence," she responded lifelessly. "You phoned him, too, from the laboratory. We know about that, as well."

If he was surprised, he didn't show it. "I called him because I wanted him to stay away from you. He wouldn't listen. Our meeting at Henshaw's was an accident, he was arriving just as I was leaving. He taunted me, said he could have you back anytime he wanted. He said other things, too, but I don't care to repeat those. Ask the man you hired to take photographs what happened that day. Stanhope and I nearly got into a fistfight. If you don't believe me, ask that private investigator you and Jerry hired."

Everything within Julia wanted to believe him. Her heart yearned to trust him. It was like an old tape being played back again and the memories it stirred to the surface were too compelling to ignore.

"This man is slime. I won't have him anywhere near you," Alek said heatedly. "If you want to condemn me for protecting you as is my duty as your husband, then you may. But I would rather rip out my own heart than hurt you."

He was saying everything Julia desperately longed to hear. She hesitated, not knowing what to do. She pressed her hands to her head and closed her eyes. "I need time to think."

He nodded, seeming to accept that, but he was hurt and she felt his pain as strongly as she did her own.

Rather than continue a discussion that would cause them both grief, she showered and dressed for bed.

Alek appeared in the doorway to the guest bedroom when she'd finished. "Anna left you dinner."

"I'm not hungry."

"You're too thin already. Eat."

"Alek, please, I'm exhausted."

"Eat," he insisted.

Julia's appetite was gone. She'd thrown up her lunch and hadn't eaten since. Unwilling to argue with him, she traipsed into the kitchen, took the foil-covered dinner plate warming in the oven and sat down at the table.

His sister had cooked veal cutlets, small red potatoes and what looked like a purple cabbage stir-fry. Even after sitting in the oven for hours, the dinner was delicious. Julia intended on sampling only a few bites to appease Alek, and then dumping the rest in the garbage disposal, but she ended up downing a respectable amount of food. When she'd finished, she rinsed off her plate and retired in the master bedroom where Alek was waiting for her.

In the morning, Julia woke to the sounds of Anna and Alek talking in the kitchen. They were speaking in Russian and it was apparent Anna was upset.

Donning her robe, Julia wandered into the other room and poured herself a cup of coffee. Anna eyed her with open hostility.

"My brother would not do this thing," she said forcefully.

"Anna," Alek barked. "Enough."

"He loves you. How can you think he would ever hurt you? He is a man of honor."

"It isn't as simple as it seems," Julia said in her own defense. Anna didn't understand, and she didn't expect she would.

Alek said something sharp and cold in his own language, but that didn't stop Anna from turning to Julia once more. "You do not know my brother, otherwise you wouldn't believe he would do this terrible thing."

"Anna," Alek continued and harshly reprimanded his sister. Julia didn't need to understand Russian to know what he was saying.

Anna responded by ripping the apron from her waist, slamming it down on the kitchen counter and storming out of the apartment.

"I apologize for my sister's behavior," Alek said after she'd left. He was so formal, so stiff and proud. He seemed to hesitate, as if trying to find the words to express himself. "There is a meeting with the marketing people this afternoon. It is a very important discussion. I need to be there to explain and answer questions. If you'd rather I wasn't, I'll try to find someone to take my place."

Julia was incapable of making the simplest decision.

"I suggest you attend it yourself. If you feel I am doing or saying anything that would hurt Conrad Industries, then you can stop me. I suggest Jerry be there, as well."

"Alek, I believe you, please try to understand how awkward this is."

"Come to the meeting," he suggested.

"All right," Julia agreed reluctantly.

He listed the time and place, and afterward the room went silent, the lack of sound punctuated by the heavy beat of their heartache. Julia heard it as clearly as the chimes from the anniversary clock that had once belonged to her parents. She was sure Alek did, too. He waited a moment, then turned and vacated the condo.

Julia was left to her own devices. Rarely had she ever felt more alone. It was as if a gaping hole had formed in her heart and nothing was capable of filling it. For the rest of her natural life she would walk around as one of the living dead. Unable to trust, unsure of herself, lost and lonely.

Her thoughts depressed her. She dressed, determined to continue on as best she could until they resolved this problem.

It wasn't until she was sitting behind the desk in her office that she made a decision, her first sensible one since this whole nightmare began.

She reached for the telephone book, swallowed tightly, praying she could pull this off, and then, with a bravado she didn't feel, she dialed Roger Stanhope's phone number.

"Mr. Stanhope's office," came the efficient reply.

"This is Julia Conrad for Mr. Stanhope."

"One moment please."

A short time passed before Roger's silky smooth voice came over the wire. "Julia, what a pleasant surprise."

"I understand you met with my husband." Preliminary greetings were unnecessary.

"So you heard about that?"

"Alek told me. I'm calling you for your own protection. Alek meant what he said about you staying away from me. If you value your neck, I don't advise you to try to contact me again." Her heart was in her throat and pounding so hard and fast she was sure he must be able to hear it.

"I think there must be some misunderstanding," Roger said with genuine incredulity. "I did meet with your husband. Actually, he was the one who contacted me, but your name didn't come into the conversation. He wanted to talk to me about Phoenix Paints. It seemed he was hoping the two of us could strike some kind of deal. Naturally Ideal Paints is very interested."

"Good try, Roger, but it won't work."

He laughed that sick, slightly demented laugh of his, as though he'd said something hilarious, certainly something worthy of amusement.

"I guess we'll just have to wait and see, won't we?" he added sarcastically.

Julia hung up the phone. His comment was gut-wrenching, all right, but it wasn't laughter that came to her.

She didn't know how long she sat there with her hand on the telephone receiver. When she found the strength, she stood, walked out of her office and directly past her secretary's desk.

"Ms. Conrad, are you feeling all right? You're terribly pale again."

Julia looked to the matronly woman who had worked for her father before her and slowly shook her head. "I'll feel all right in a few minutes, I'm sure."

"Have you thought about seeing a doctor?" Julia didn't know any physician who specialized in treating broken hearts. Her secretary continued to look at her, anticipating a reply. "No, I don't . . . need one."

"I think you do. I'm going to make an appointment for you and ask for the first available opening. We can't have you walking around looking as if you're going to faint at any moment."

Julia barely heard her. She walked farther into the hallway to the elevator and rode down a floor to where her brother's office was situated.

Jerry stood when she walked in. "Julia, sweet heaven, sit down, you look like you're about to keel over."

For her brother to comment, she must resemble yesterday's oatmeal. "I'm fine," she lied.

"Do you need a glass of water?"

She briefly closed her eyes and shook her head. She hadn't come to discuss her state of health.

"I'm getting you one anyway. You look dreadful."

Julia pinched her lips together to bite back a cutting commentary on her looks, and didn't succeed. "How nice of you to say so."

Jerry chuckled and left his office and returned a couple of minutes later with a paper cup filled with cool water. He insisted Julia drink it, which she did. To her surprise she felt better afterward. But then, it was impossible to feel any worse than she already did.

"I imagine you're here to find out what Alek said."

"What Alek said makes a lot of sense," Jerry continued. "He claims he confronted Roger and told him to leave you alone. I wish I'd done it myself. The man's a bastard."

"I talked to Roger myself...."

Jerry froze and his eyes narrowed suspiciously. "You talked to Roger?"

"This morning."

"What did he say?" Jerry demanded. "Never mind, I can guess." He started pacing then as if holding still was impossible just then. "Naturally he wasn't going to tell you Alek threatened him within an inch of his life. What did you expect him to say? That he was shaking in his boots with fear? The man wouldn't know the truth if it hit him along the side of the head. How could you do anything so stupid?"

"I . . ."

"I thought you were smarter than this."

"Roger claims Alek tried to strike a deal with our strongest competitor for Phoenix Paints," Julia said, trying hard to hold on to her temper.

"I don't believe that for a minute."

Neither did Julia, but she was so desperately afraid. She needed Jerry to confirm her belief in Alek, needed the reassurance that she wasn't making the same tragic mistake a second time.

"Don't you realize you're playing directly into Roger's hands? This is exactly what he was looking to happen. You certainly made his day."

"I . . . hadn't thought of it like that," Julia admitted reluctantly. She was a fool not to leave the detective work to Rich Peck.

"You contacted Roger even knowing the kind of man he is, and expected him to tell the truth. You've done some stupid things in your time, Julia, but this one takes the cake."

Julia bristled. "The cake came three years ago, Jerry," she reminded him. "Complete with frosting, don't you remember? That was when I trusted Roger, when I believed in love and loyalty."

"You believe Alek, don't you?"

"Of course."

Jerry's eyes narrowed. "Then why'd you contact Roger?"

"Because I hoped...I don't know, I thought he might let something slip."

"He did that, all right, another truckload of doubts for you to deal with." He rammed his hand through his hair. "I can't believe you'd do anything so asinine."

"I wish you'd quit saying that."

"It's true. Now are you going to believe in Alek or aren't you?"

With all her heart, she wanted to trust her husband, but she'd been hurt badly before. She'd zealously defended Roger, even when faced with overwhelming proof. Her faith in him had nearly destroyed her family. She rested her hands against her forehead and briefly closed her eyes.

"I take it you didn't fire him, then?"

"No. I won't, either. If you want him out of here, then you're going to have to do it yourself. I believe him, Julia, even if you don't."

"Jerry, please, try and understand this is like waking up to my worst nightmare. Don't you think I want to believe him? I do so damn much it's killing me."

"I can see that. Just let it be for now, Julia. Time will tell if he's being honest with us or not."

"I can't let the fate of the company ride on your gut instinct. I don't feel I have any choice but to ask for his resignation."

Jerry's fist clenched at his side. "You can't do that."

"I'm the president of this company, I can do as I damn well please." She didn't want to get hard-nosed about this, but her first obligation was to protect their family business. Jerry was silent as he absorbed her words. "So you're going to pull rank on me."

Although Julia was the acting president, Jerry was her brother and invaluable to the company. "I didn't mean it like that. The last thing we need to do is argue with one another."

"If you ask Alek to go..."

"Jerry, please, I have to, don't you see?"

"If you ask for Alek's resignation," he started again, "you'll receive mine, as well."

Julia felt as if her own brother had kicked her in the stomach. "It's funny," she said unemotionally, "I remember saying those very same words to Dad three years ago. I believed Roger, remember...of course you do, how could you not?"

"A week," Jerry said. "We'll know more in another few days. All I ask is that you give him the opportunity to prove himself."

"As I recall, I said something along those lines to Dad, too."

"Alek isn't Roger," Jerry said forcefully. "What's it going to take to prove that to you?"

"I know that," she agreed vehemently. "Maybe it would be best if I was the one who resigned."

"Don't be ridiculous. Just give this thing time. If Alek sold us out, then there's nothing we can do about it now. The deed's done. It isn't going to hurt us any to sit on our doubts for the next several days. Promise me you'll do that."

"The longer he's here, the more he'll learn."

"So? He could anyway."

"All right," Julia said angrily. "I'll give it another week, but then it's over, Jerry. Alek goes and I can go back to running this company the way it's supposed to be done.

Jerry's smile was fleeting. "I promise you, it's going to be different this time."

She stood to leave, then recalled her conversation with her husband that morning. "Alek mentioned an important meeting with marketing this afternoon." She gave Jerry the particulars. "He said he'd like us both there. Can you make it?"

Jerry flipped the pages of his appointment calendar and nodded. "With a bit of juggling. You're going, too?"

"Yes," she said, but she wasn't looking forward to it.

Alek waited for Julia and Jerry to arrive. He watched the door, anticipating their coming. Jerry was the first one to show and he walked into the conference room and took the chair next to Alek.

"You talked to her?" Alek didn't need to explain who he meant.

Jerry nodded. "I've never seen her like this. This thing is tearing her apart."

"It hasn't been easy on any of us. I wish I knew what to do to clear my name. Julia would barely listen to me. It was as though she curled up into a tight ball and blocked everything and everyone out, including me."

"It would be a hell of a lot easier if she were a man."

Alek arched his brows and laughed for the first time in days. "No, it wouldn't."

"For making her listen to reason it would. Sometimes I forget my sister is a woman—she clouds the issues with emotions."

Personally Alek had no trouble remembering Julia was female. "Not all women have been betrayed the way she was," he said. "I understand her fears, but at the same time I want her to believe me because she loves and knows me enough to realize I'd never do anything to hurt either of you. Until she does, there's nothing I can do."

"I don't know what Julia believes anymore and she doesn't either," Jerry said after a moment. "I talked her into giving the matter a week."

"A week," Alek repeated. "Nothing can happen in that time. The paints won't hit the market for another two to three weeks at the earliest."

"There's a good deal more to consider from her end of things," Jerry said sadly.

"She's miserable," Alek added, although he suffered the same symptoms. "She doesn't eat properly, she's working herself to death and she's sleeping poorly, too." In truth he wasn't in much better shape himself. There was nothing he could say in his own defense that would make her believe him.

He loved Julia, but he couldn't force her to trust him, he couldn't demand that she believe him. She would have to reach those decisions for herself. In the meantime he was left helpless and hopeless, and worst of all, defenseless. She was judging him on her experience with another man, one who had hurt and betrayed her.

"Damn, but I thought Stanhope was out of our lives once and for all. If anyone is a fool, it's me. I should have calculated he'd be back when we're on the brink of a major product breakthrough. We should have been better prepared."

"No one could have known."

"I should have," Jerry said, his lips thinning with irritation. "Only this time Roger knows he doesn't have a chance of stealing anything, so he's undermining our trust in each other."

The marketing people arrived with their displays. Most of what they'd be reviewing was geared toward television and radio advertising. The magazine ads had been done a month or so earlier and would be coming out in the latest monthly issues of fifteen major publications.

The advertising executive glanced at his watch. Alek sighed. Jerry echoed the sentiment. Everyone in the room was waiting for Julia.

"Virginia, please, I have a meeting with marketing."

"But I have Dr. Feldon's office on the line. If you could wait just a few minutes."

Julia glanced pointedly at her watch while her secretary haggled for the first opening in Dr. Feldon's already full appointment schedule.

"That'll be fine, I'll be sure she's there. Thank you for your helpfulness."

"Well?" Julia said, after her secretary replaced the telephone receiver.

"Five o'clock. The doctor has agreed to squeeze you in then."

Julia nodded. She wished now that she'd put her foot down, so to speak, over this appointment issue. A doctor wasn't going to be able to tell her anything she didn't already know. She was suffering from stress and tension, which, given her circumstances, was understandable. A psychiatrist would have been a better choice. The best she could hope for was a prescription of tranquilizers from Dr. Feldon, and she doubted that she'd have it filled.

"You won't forget now, will you?" her secretary called after her as Julia headed for the elevator.

"No, I'll be there. Thank you for your trouble."

"You do what Dr. Feldon says, you hear? We can't have you getting sick every afternoon now, can we?"

Julia grinned. Virginia was beginning to sound like a mother hen. "I'll see you in the morning," Julia answered. "Why don't you take an early afternoon?" she suggested. "You deserve it for putting up with me."

Her secretary looked mildly surprised, then nodded. "Thank you, I will."

It seemed every head turned when a breathless Julia burst into the conference room. "I'm sorry I'm late," she said, sitting in the chair closest to the door.

The marketing director smiled benignly and walked over to a television set that had been brought in for the demonstration. "I thought we'd start with the media blitz scheduled to be aired a week from this Thursday," he said as he inserted a videotape into the VCR.

Julia couldn't help being aware of Alek. His eyes were on her from the moment she'd entered the room. She expected to feel the brunt of his anger, instead she felt his love. Tears clogged her throat. It would have been easier for her if she'd found him with another woman than to learn he'd been talking to Roger, no matter what the reason.

"Our agency is very pleased with the effectiveness of this twenty-second advertisement."

The figure of a man and a woman came onto the screen. The husband was on a ladder painting the side of the house. The woman was working on the lawn below, painting a patio table with four matching chairs. Two children played serenely on a swing set in the background. The music was a classical piece she recognized but couldn't have named. The announcer's well-modulated voice came on but for the life of her Julia couldn't hear what was being said.

The room started to spin. The light fixtures faded in and out as though someone were controlling a dimmer switch. She thought she heard someone cry out but even that seemed to be coming from a long way away.

When she regained consciousness, Julia found herself on the floor. She blinked up at the ceiling. Alek was crouched over her, his arm supporting the back of her neck. His eyes were filled with anxiety.

"What happened?" she asked.

"You fainted," Jerry supplied. He was kneeling down beside her, holding on to her hand, patting it gently. "I'll say this for you, Julia, you certainly know how to get a man's heart going. You keeled right over."

"Where is everyone?"

"We had them leave. Alek and I will review the video later."

"I don't understand it," she said, struggling into a sitting position. "One moment I was perfectly fine and the next thing I knew the room started whirling."

"Get her some water," Alek instructed.

Jerry left the room and Alek wrapped his arm around her back, helped her into an upright sitting position and held her against his chest. She braced her hands against his ribs, intending on pushing herself free.

"No," he said, kissing her temple. "You can mistrust and hate me later, but for right now let me hold you."

"That's the problem," she whispered. "I believe you."

"You know so little Julia. Now, we won't speak of this again. You've worked yourself into a state of collapse."

"I don't know what happened here, but I'm sure it's nothing important. I've just been overly stressed, is all. We all have been."

Jerry returned with the water. "Why is it I'm always getting you water?" he said jokingly, handing her a paper cup. "My goodness, you'd think I'd gone to college to be a water boy instead of an attorney."

"I'm sorry," she said, pressing her hand to the side of her head. "I didn't mean to create such a commotion."

"Should we take her back to the office?" Jerry asked, looking to Alek.

"No, I'll take her home."

"If you don't mind, I prefer to make my own decisions," Julia stiffly informed them both. They made it sound as if she were a piece of furniture they couldn't decide where to place.

Bracing her hand against the back of the chair, she stood. She felt a bit unstable, but that dizziness quickly passed. "I'm fine. You two go about your business and I'll go about mine."

"Julia, for the love of heaven, would you kindly listen to common sense? You just fainted," Jerry informed her, as if she hadn't figured it out yet.

"I know what happened."

"Let Alek take you home."

"No."

"I think she'd feel more comfortable if you took her," Alek suggested.

"I fainted," she told both men, "I didn't have a lobotomy. Let me assure you, I'm perfectly capable of making my own decisions, and I'm not leaving this office until I'm finished with what I need to do."

"Some of those decisions should be questioned," Jerry snapped, sounding furious.

"Jerry."

"Shut up, Alek, this is between me and my sister. She's an emotional and physical wreck because of all of this and to complicate matters she decides to play detective herself."

"I don't understand."

"Jerry, do you mind if we discuss this another time?" Julia said.

"No. Alek has a right to know. Tell him."

"Julia?" Alek turned to face her. "What's Jerry talking about?"

She flashed her brother a scathing look. "It's nothing."

"Fine, I'll tell him. Julia had the bright idea of calling Roger herself and playing this crazy truth game with him. She said she knew about the meeting between the two of you and that you meant what you'd said about staying away from her."

Alek's gaze narrowed. "And what did Stanhope say?"

"You can well imagine."

"I didn't believe Roger," Julia said in her own defense. "I never did." Jerry was right, contacting Roger hadn't been the smartest thing she'd ever done, but she was desperate.

"What my sister failed to remember is that Roger isn't stupid. She was fishing for information and he knew it, so he made up this ridiculous story about you trying to strike a deal with Ideal Paints."

Alek released a one-word expletive.

"It's eating her up inside," Jerry continued. "She was as pale as egg white when she came to see me this morning."

Julia watched her husband. He was distancing himself from her, both emotionally and physically. Almost before her eyes, he erected a cold front, freezing her out.

"She must make her own decision and I must make mine." Without another word, Alek turned and left the conference room.

"I wish you hadn't said anything to him about my talk with Roger."

"Why not? He had a right to know."

Her lack of faith had hurt Alek. She'd seen it in his eyes and in the way he'd stiffened and moved away from her. Covering her face with her hands, Julia slowly exhaled and her breath came out in small wobbles like a young bird cooing for its mother.

"I have to go," she whispered. "I'll talk to you in the morning."

Julia's head was pounding as she walked out of the conference room. She checked the time, wanting to know how long it was before her appointment with Dr. Feldon. The physician had been treating her family for the past fifteen years and knew Julia well.

She arrived at his office at one minute past five and was ushered directly into the cubical. His nurse asked her a variety of questions.

"Basically, I've been under a good deal of stress lately," Julia explained. "This afternoon the craziest thing happened. I fainted. Me! I can't believe it."

After taking her temperature and her blood pressure, Dr. Feldon's nurse asked for a urine sample.

Only a matter of minutes passed before she was joined by Dr. Feldon. His hair was grayer than the last time she was in to see him and he was a little thicker about the waist.

"Julia, it's good to see you, although I wish it were under different circumstances. Now tell me what's the problem."

The tears came as a surprise and an acute embarrassment. "I . . . I'm just not myself lately. There's been so much happening with the company and I've been under a good deal of stress, and to make matters worse I fainted right in the middle of a marketing meeting and gave my husband and my brother the scare of their lives."

Dr. Feldon reached for a tissue and pressed it into her hand. "How are you feeling now?"

She had to stop and think about it. "A little woozy."

"And emotional?"

She nodded eagerly, paused and then blew her nose.

"I'd say this is all normal, my dear. Most pregnant women are known to suffer these symptoms."

Chapter Twelve

"Pregnant?" Julia repeated in a shocked whisper. "You mean all this, the nausea and the fainting spell, is happening because I'm going to have a baby?"

"No, I think the stress you've talked about is complicating the symptoms."

"But I don't have morning sickness."

"A good many women don't. Several have been known to suffer from afternoon sickness. My guess is that you're one of these fortunate few."

"I should have realized...." Julia whispered, surprised she hadn't realized her condition much sooner, herself.

"As you probably know I gave up delivering babies several years back. I can recommend an excellent colleague of mine who's been making quite a name for herself. I'll have my receptionist make an appointment for you, if you'd like. Her name is Dr. Lois Brandt and my patients who've had babies delivered by her have been very pleased."

"Yes, that would be fine." Julia was both excited and shocked, although heaven knew she had no right to be. "How... far along do you think I am?"

Dr. Feldon chuckled. "My guess is about two weeks."

She nodded, knowing it couldn't be much more than that, amazed, too, that her pregnancy could be detected so early.

"I'm going to prescribe prenatal vitamins and have you start watching your diet. According to those ridiculous charts the insurance companies put out, you're about five pounds underweight. Don't skip meals, and make an effort to eat from the five major food groups every day with plenty of fresh fruits and vegetables."

Julia nodded eagerly. Dr. Feldon made it sound as if she were pregnant with a rabbit instead of a baby.

She left the office a few minutes later, her step lighter. A baby. She was going to have a baby. Alek would...

Alek.

Her thoughts came to a skidding halt. This compounded everything tenfold. Far more was at stake now than before. Much more was involved. They'd introduced a tiny being into the equation.

Julia's steps slowed. She wasn't sure what to do or say to him, if anything. At least, not yet. He had a right to know, but Julia wasn't convinced now was the time to tell him. My heavens, she'd gotten herself into something of a predicament.

She returned to her condominium and let herself inside. Two steps into the entryway and she nearly stumbled over a large leather suitcase.

She heard movements in the master bedroom and walked down the hallway leading to the room. Alek stood just inside the walk-in closet, carefully removing his clothes from the thick pine hangers. Another large leather suitcase yawned opened on top of the mattress.

"Alek? What are you doing?"

He continued as if he hadn't heard her. "It should be obvious."

"You're moving out," she whispered and the words hit her in the face like a slap of icy rain. Alek was leaving.

"I knew you'd figure it out sooner or later." He walked over to his suitcase and carefully folded his shirts and placed them inside.

"Where will you be living?"

"I don't know yet. I don't believe there's any reason for us to stay in contact after I move out."

"What about at the office, I mean . . ."

"As of four-thirty this afternoon I am no longer an employee of Conrad Industries."

An icy hand wrapped itself around Julia's heart at the connotation. "I see . . . you're going to work for Ideal Paints."

He turned around to face her so fast, she felt a draft. "No, Julia, I'm not going to work for the competition. I know it means nothing to you, but the Berinski word of honor is all I have to offer you as proof. On the blood of my father, I assure you that I would never do anything to hurt you or Jerry. That includes betraying you to Ideal Paints or any other of your competitors." He spun back around and resumed his task, his movements abrupt and hurried as if he was eager to be on his way. Julia didn't want him to leave, but she couldn't ask him to stay, either.

"Why now?" she asked, sitting on the edge of the mattress. She wasn't sure her legs would continue to support her much longer. She felt as if she was about to break into tears, which would have embarrassed them both.

"I'd hoped that given time you'd recognize the truth, but I don't believe that's possible any longer."

"Why not?" She was beginning to sound like a parrot seeking a cracker, but she couldn't help it.

"If you believe Stanhope's word over mine, then I have to accept that you're not capable of recognizing the truth when you hear it."

Julia had no argument to give him, although the doubts were beginning to mount more each moment. "Are you going to want a divorce?"

He went still, as if the question required some consideration. "That's up to you. I told you once that my religion forbids it."

Julia relaxed a little, but not much.

"But I can't live with you, Julia, and I can't see ever living with you again."

"It wasn't so bad, was it?" she said, looking for something, anything to bring them back together, to force him to acknowledge his love for her. Telling him her news was tempting, but if he stayed, she wanted it to be because he loved her and not because she'd trapped him with the news of a baby.

"No, Julia, living with you wasn't bad, if you don't mind a porcupine for a wife."

She sucked in her breath at the pain his words caused.

His shoulders sagged as he exhaled sharply. "I shouldn't have said that. I apologize."

"I've hurt you, too."

He didn't respond, but she knew she had, unintentionally. He was intent on his task, and refused to look up at her. He closed the lid to the suitcase, locked it, then dragged it from the mattress. He carried it into the other room and set it next to the first suitcase.

"If you forget anything, where would you like me to send it?" she asked, hoping to appear helpful when she was actually looking for a means of keeping in contact with him.

He frowned, then said, "Give it to Anna. She'll know where I am."

"I . . . think you might be acting a bit hastily, don't you? Why don't you give it some thought?" This was as far as she was willing to go. She wouldn't ask him to stay, wouldn't plead with him or make an issue of his going. Those choices were his.

"There's nothing to think about," he told her with such stiff pride that the words sounded as if they'd been drenched in starch. "Goodbye, Julia." He added something softly in Russian, opened the door, reached for his suitcases and walked out of the condominium and her life.

Julia stood for a moment, so stunned and feeling so bereft that she couldn't move. Or breathe. Or think. The abilities returned slowly, one by one. Unhurriedly she turned and moved into the living room, collapsing onto the white leather sofa.

She'd had one hell of a day. Within the space of a few hours, she'd fainted, learned she was pregnant and had her husband move out on her. The prospects for the future didn't look any brighter, either.

The phone rang fifteen minutes later and Julia grabbed it, thinking, praying it was Alek. "Hello," she answered eagerly.

"Julia, have you seen Alek? Listen, you've got to talk some sense into him. I just got back to my office and discovered his letter of resignation. What do you know about this? Listen, don't answer that, just put him on the line, I'll convince him he's overreacting."

"I can't," she said, biting into her lower lip. "I really wish I could, but you see, Alek doesn't live here anymore."

"What do you mean?"

"He moved out. I found him packing when I arrived home."

"Why the hell didn't you stop him?"

"How?"

"Oh, I don't know," Jerry said with heavy sarcasm. "Maybe you could have told him you believe in him and trust him. You might have thanked him for working two long years on the project that's destined to take this company's profit line right off the page. You could have even told him you love him and didn't want him to go."

Julia, who was softly crying by then, sniffled. "Yeah, I guess I could."

"Do you believe him now?"

"I...don't know, but I think I do, because not trusting him hurts too damn much."

Jerry swore under his breath and then sighed loudly. "You've got one a hell of a sense of timing. Did anyone ever tell you that?"

"No," she said, wiping the moisture away from her cheek.

"Go to him, Julia," Jerry advised, "before it's too late."

"It is too late," she whispered. "I don't know where he is and he didn't want to tell me."

The following morning, Julia was waiting for Anna when the woman arrived. "Good morning, Anna."

Alek's sister frowned and didn't respond. She walked over to the broom closet, brought out her apron and tied it around her waist, all the while ignoring Julia.

"I guess you heard that Alek moved out?" she asked, following her sister-in-law.

Still Anna didn't acknowledge her. She opened the refrigerator and brought out a dozen eggs.

"Do you know where he is?"

"Of course, he is my brother."

"Would you mind telling me?"

"So you can hurt him more? So you can think terrible things of him? So you can accuse his honor? No, I will not tell you anything about my brother."

"I love him," Julia whispered. "I've just been so afraid. You see, three years ago I loved a man who betrayed my family and me. I believed him when I shouldn't have. I defended him and my father and I got in a terrible argument and my father... while we were fighting he suffered a heart attack. He died and I felt so incredibly guilty. I blamed myself." Anna had turned to face Julia, her face white and emotionless. "Can you understand why it's so difficult to believe Alek? Can you see why I'm skeptical after all the things that have happened?" Tears were very close to the surface, but she held them back, wadding a tissue in her hand until it was a small white ball.

"My brother would never betray you."

"I know that. I've always known that."

"Alek isn't this other man."

"I know that, too, but I made a mistake and gave Alek reason to believe I doubted him." She stopped, realizing that arguing her case with Alek's sister wasn't going to help.

She dressed for work with no enthusiasm. In another ten days, Phoenix Paints would be available to the public. Conrad Industries would be the first to break into a whole new market for paint and paint products, thanks to her father's dream and Alek's genius. Somehow it all seemed empty now. The purpose that had driven her all these years meant nothing without Alek at her side.

Jerry was waiting in her office for her. "Did you find out where he's staying?"

Julia shook her head. "His sister wouldn't tell me. I don't blame her. If our positions were reversed, I wouldn't tell her, either."

"I'll get Rich on it right away."

"No," she said softly. "Leave Alek his pride. I've robbed him of everything else." She walked around her desk and sat down. Reaching for her desk calendar, she flipped the pages ahead eight months. "I'm going to need some extensive time off soon."

"We all need a vacation, Julia."

"This is going to be more than a two-week vacation, Jerry. I'm going to need maternity leave."

* * *

Alek sat at the table in the library and marveled at the rows upon rows of information readily available to those who wished it. He wondered why there wasn't a line waiting for admission. He'd attended a Mariner baseball game and waited fifteen minutes before he was able to purchase his ticket. It didn't make sense to him that the people of Seattle loved baseball more than books.

Perhaps that was his problem. He knew more of books than people. He had badly bungled his marriage. It had been over a week since he'd last seen Julia. Two weeks since he'd moved out of their condominium—her condominium, he corrected.

He'd seen her interviewed on a local television station the day Phoenix Paints hit the market. She looked pale and so beautiful he hadn't been able to take his eyes off the television screen. Long after her sweet face had vanished from view, he'd continued to stare at the television as if he were a lovesick puppy.

She'd answered the reporter's questions, told about her father's vision for the paint industry and how Alek had seen it to fruition. Alek had been surprised that she'd mentioned his name, credited him with the innovations. Paints that changed color, paints developed for easy removal, paints that were guaranteed to last into the next generation.

Alek thought long and hard about what she'd said, wondering if she was trying to tell him something. If she had, he'd lost the meaning. He was worried about her; she looked drained, but jubilant. Jerry was at her side and had fielded several of the questions.

Alek closed the book he was reading. He relied on Anna for information about Julia, but his sister had gotten stubborn of late, refusing to give him the detailed answers he sought. She seemed to think if he was so curious, he should talk to his wife himself.

Alek rolled the suggestion around in his mind. He'd left because he couldn't tolerate the thought of her mistrust.

His gaze fell to his swollen, bruised knuckles and he flexed his hand. Standing, he returned the book to the shelf and reached for his jacket. It was raining outside, misty and miserable. It didn't make sense to carry an umbrella but his hair was drenched by the time he'd gone a single block.

It was while he was passing a large parked van that he caught the reflection in the side mirror of a man in a beige raincoat behind him. It was the same man he'd seen in the library. Alek wondered. It would be foolish to believe he was being followed. Then again, he'd lived in a country where it was not uncommon for citizens to disappear for no reason and never be heard from again.

He stepped into an alley and waited. The man casually strolled past and continued down the walkway. Alek expelled his breath, thinking he'd become fanciful. Then again, it wouldn't be beneath Stanhope to hire someone to injure him.

Alek grinned at the memory of the other man. No, he decided, Stanhope was just the type to have someone else do his dirty work for him.

Alek walked for several blocks until he reached the Seattle waterfront. It had become one of his favorites. The fish-and-chips were excellent and there was a covered eating space along the pier. He hadn't eaten since breakfast, so he purchased a double order and carried it out onto the farthest end of the dock. Here he could look out over the water and view the nautical activity on Puget Sound. He claimed a blue picnic table and sat down to enjoy his dinner.

He was lost in his thoughts apparently, because he didn't notice the man in the raincoat until he was almost on top of him.

"I guess I better sit down and introduce myself," the man said. He held out his hand. "The name's Rich Peck."

Alek stood and the two exchanged handshakes. "Hello."

"You figured out I was following you, didn't you?" Uninvited, Peck sat down at the table, across from Alek.

Alek shrugged. "I had my suspicions."

"Damn," Peck muttered, "I must be getting sloppy."

"There was a reason you've been tracking my movements?"

Peck grinned, that cocky grin Alek saw often in American men. It was a make-my-day look. "There generally is a reason. This time someone's paying me. Rather handsomely, I might add. Cushy jobs like this aren't easy to come by."

Alek was more confused than ever. "Roger Stanhope paid you to follow me?"

"Stanhope. Don't count on it. The man hasn't got two dimes to rub together. Oh, by the way, I heard about your little skirmish with him. Provoking him into taking the first swing was smart. I heard he tried to hit you from behind. The man's a sleaze. Are you pressing assault charges against him?"

"No, I figured I'd punished him enough. I know one thing for sure, he'll stay out of Julia's life now. He knows what will happen to him if he doesn't."

"Listen, Stanhope's got more problems than you know," Peck went on to say. "He'll be happy to stay away from anything to do with Conrad Industries for the next fifteen years. If he lives that long, which I personally doubt. He borrowed money from the wrong kind of people, if you know what I mean."

"You know a lot about this slime ball."

Peck shrugged. "I was paid to learn what I could. The guy is an open book. You, on the other hand, weren't so easy to track down. Your sister wouldn't tell me a thing. She pretended she didn't understand English."

"Who hired you to follow me?" Alek was growing bored with this detailed speech.

"Sorry, but that's privileged information."

"Julia?" His heart pounded hard with excitement.

"Nope. Anyway, my lips are sealed. But I can tell you it isn't her. She doesn't know anything about this, although what I'm supposed to tell you involves her."

Alek was beginning to think he didn't like Peck as much as he had in the beginning. "Then tell me."

Peck arched his twin brows at Alek's less than patient tone. "First, let me ask you a couple of questions."

"I don't have time for this." Alek surged to his feet and stalked away. He half expected Peck to follow him, but when the private investigator didn't, he slowed his pace.

Alek had gone a block before he recognized his mistake. His impatience had cost him what he'd wanted most, information about Julia. He turned back, walking at a fast clip. He need not have worried; Peck was sitting at the table, enjoying the fish-and-chips dinner Alek had hastily left behind.

Alek stood over him and Peck licked his fingers. "I thought you might have a change of heart."

"Tell me."

"No problem, big boy. Jerry thought there was something you'd like to know about his sister. She's going to be a mother. If I understand this correctly, that means you're about to become a daddy."

Alek felt as if he'd had his legs knocked out from under him. He literally slumped into the picnic table. "When?"

"I can't answer that one. I don't think she's very far along. A month, maybe two."

"Have you seen her? Is she healthy?"

Peck shrugged. "The last time I did, she was a little green around the gills."

These crazy American idioms. "Green gills? What does that mean?"

"You know, a little under the weather."

Alek's confusion increased. "Say it in plain English, please."

"Okay, okay. She's as sick as a dog every afternoon. Jerry says it's like watching Old Faithful. About three-fifteen her secretary leads her to the ladies' room so she can lose her lunch. It's perfectly normal from what I understand. Not that I know much about pregnant women."

Alek felt as if someone were sitting on his chest and the weight kept increasing. A baby. Julia was going to have his baby.

He stood once more and frowned. By heaven, he had a right to know and the news shouldn't have come from his brother-in-law, either. Julia should have told him herself.

A low, burning anger simmered in his blood. He was angry, angrier than he could ever remember being before, and he wasn't about to let it go. Not this time.

"You tell Jerry something for me," Alek growled.

"Sure."

He paused. He didn't have any cause to be angry with Jerry. His friend had taken the initiative and sent Peck to tell him what he should have been told from the beginning.

"You wanted me to pass something along to Jerry?" Peck pressed.

"Yeah," Alek said, feeling the beginnings of a smile. "Tell him I think he's going to make one hell of an uncle."

Julia took another bite of celery and set it alongside of her dinner plate. Her attention wavered from the text book for only an instant while she reached for a slice of apple.

The manual, one she'd recently picked up at the bookstore, listed the stages of pregnancy week by exciting week. She kept the book hidden from Anna, and brought it out in the evenings. By the time Junior was ready to be born, she'd practically have the whole three hundred pages memorized.

She called the baby Junior, although she hadn't a clue if it was a boy or a girl. Funny, only a couple of weeks ago she hadn't even known she was pregnant, and now it seemed as though the baby had always been a part of her.

At night, she slept with her hand flattened against her stomach. She talked to Junior, carrying on lengthy conversations with her unborn child, telling him about her day and how much she missed his or her father.

Jerry and Virginia had turned into small-time terrorists. Julia swore her secretary suffered more with her bouts of afternoon sickness than Julia did herself. And Jerry. She smiled as she thought about her brother and how solicitous he had become of late. He was constantly asking after her health. He'd even gone so far as to contact Dr. Feldon about her daily bouts of afternoon sickness.

She had been in to see Dr. Brandt and liked the young, attractive woman very much. They'd talked at length and Julia understood far better the changes that were taking place within her body. What surprised her the most was her breasts. They'd been tender at first and now they seemed to be growing firmer and—she hated to admit it—larger. It was a change Alek would have appreciated.

Alek.

She tried not to think about him, tried not to dwell on how much she missed him. Or the mistakes she made in her brief marriage. Sooner or later she'd need to get in touch with him. If for nothing more than to beg his forgiveness and thank him. Phoenix Paints had taken the market by storm. A national television network had called wanting to do a news piece on the ideas behind the innovative paints.

She owed Alek so much and she'd treated him so poorly.

She hadn't asked Anna about his whereabouts since that first morning. His sister didn't volunteer any information about Alek even when Julia asked. Julia didn't think Anna had yet forgiven her for hurting her brother.

She pressed her hand to her stomach and whispered, "Your daddy is a wonderful man, Junior. He's going to love you so much."

She took another bite of the celery stalk and turned the page of her text. Labor and delivery. She'd read this chapter first, the same night she bought the book, wanting to know everything she could about the subject. Horror stories about the birthing process had abounded for years. Tales of fifty-hour labors, and other myths of torture.

When she did deliver Junior, she hoped that Alek would be there to coach her. From what she'd seen of Jerry, he wouldn't last ten minutes in a delivery room. And Virginia, her dear sweet maiden secretary, wouldn't be able to take the pain, Julia was convinced of that.

When she'd finished with her snack, Julia moved into the living room to exercise. She turned on the television and inserted the low-impact aerobics tape into the VCR. Ten minutes later she was huffing and puffing and sweating enough to drench the gray T-shirt she wore.

"I hope you appreciate this," she told the baby.

After a full thirty minutes, she moved into the kitchen, took down a glass from the cupboard and gulped some water down. As soon as she'd finished, she grabbed a pencil and marked the schedule posted on the refrigerator front. Anna thought it was a diet sheet and it was. Sort of. Julia listed the food she ate, plus her water intake. Eight glasses a day, no excuses.

This was another interesting aspect of her condition. Her life was now ruled by how long it would take her to reach a bathroom. She'd toyed with having one installed in her office because it was so disruptive to have to hurry down the hall every fifteen minutes, and sometimes less. The eight glasses of water didn't help matters.

She was feeling better, and for that Julia was grateful. The first couple of weeks after Alek had moved out she'd felt as if she were living in a nightmare. She did what needed to be done, performed her duties, ate, worked and slept, but it was done with a black cloud hanging over her heart and with an air of expectancy. She couldn't seem to let go of the idea that Alek would come marching into her office the way he used to do. It was the promise of seeing him again, of telling him about the baby, that had kept her going.

The doorbell rang and Julia ripped the sweatband from her brow and wiped the back of her arm across her forehead. It was probably Jerry, who'd taken to checking up on her in the evenings.

But it wasn't. When she opened the door, Alek stood before her looking more furious than she could ever remember seeing him.

Chapter Thirteen

"Alek." Julia found she couldn't say anything more. He looked wonderful, while she resembled a towel that had been sitting all week at the bottom of the dirty-clothes hamper.

"I just heard you're pregnant. Is it true?" His eyes were as hard as granite. He was furious with her and didn't bother to disguise the fact.

"It's true."

"You might have told me. I played an important role in this event."

"Yes, I know, it's just that..." She realized then that she'd left him standing in the hallway outside the condo. Opening the door wider, she stepped aside. "Come inside, please."

"You weren't going to tell me about the baby?" He was frowning and furious and not the least concerned about hiding his irritation with her.

"Of course I intended to tell you."

"When?"

"Would you care to sit down?"

"No, just answer the question."

Julia ignored the demand in his voice. "Would you like something to drink?"

"Just answer the question!"

"There's no reason to yell. I was going to tell you, how could I not? This baby is as much a part of you as me. There's was never any question of my letting you know. How could I keep something this important from you?" She hoped that would appease him.

"That's my question exactly," Alek growled. His hands were knotted into fists at his sides. Julia would have liked to think he was restraining himself from holding her.

She led the way into the kitchen. He hesitated and then followed her. She poured him a glass of water and then another for herself and set them both down on the kitchen table.

"Anna knew?"

"No. I couldn't tell her for fear she'd say something to you." Her explanation didn't satisfy him any; if anything, his scowl darkened.

Julia pulled out a chair and sat. Alek followed suit. Avoiding his probing eyes, she lowered her gaze to the sweating water glass. "I'm drinking two quarts of water every day now. Eight full glasses... I'm keeping track of my intake on the sheet on the refrigerator."

Julia didn't know why it was so important to tell him that when they had so many other things to discuss.

"The baby needs water?"

"In a manner of speaking, I guess, but actually it's me the doctor's concerned about."

"Why is the doctor worried?"

She hadn't said this to alarm Alek, but just as a matter of conversation, a way to ease the tension between them. "I'm perfectly healthy, Alek, don't look so concerned."

"Then why is your doctor troubled?"

"They're paid to show concern, it's nothing to fret over. Thus far I'm having a perfectly normal pregnancy. At least, that's what the book says." She reached across the table for the manual she'd read from cover to cover three times over. "Junior's doing just great."

"Junior?"

"That's what I call him . . . or her."

The anger had faded and in its place Julia read a love and devotion so deep that it wounded her tender heart. To think that she'd abused that love, and mistrusted his word. The knot in her throat grew impossibly thick. Tears filled her eyes.

"Julia."

She bit into her lower lip and looked away. "Don't worry, it's all part of this pregnancy thing. I'm so terribly emotional. The other night I started crying over a silly television ad." She didn't tell him it was the one for Phoenix Paints. The tears had come so fast because she'd realized how very much she missed her husband.

Alek handed her his handkerchief.

"Thanks." She dabbed her eyes. "Look on page fifty-three of the book. It'll explain why a woman's inclined to cry when she's pregnant."

Alek flipped through the pages until he found the one she mentioned. He scanned the text and nodded.

"How have you been feeling?"

She shrugged. "All right, I guess. I don't get sick in the mornings the way most women do. I usually get nauseous around three-thirty in the afternoon. I don't know why I bother to eat lunch since it comes right back up again."

"Have you had any other problems?"

"No," she was quick to assure him. "Actually, I've been feeling great. You'll be proud of me, I've been eating three square meals a day with lots of fresh fruits and vegetables." She stopped when she noticed the way he was staring at her. "Is something wrong?"

Alek's gaze left hers and he shook his head. "Never mind."

"No, tell me, please."

He hesitated and a sickening feeling attacked Julia's heart. She'd read about such things, in the very book that rested on the table between her and Alek. Some men were turned off by their wives during pregnancy.

"You are more beautiful than ever," Alek whispered.

Julia bit into her lower lip and a sigh trembled through her.

"That disappoints you?"

"I'm not beautiful, Alek. The way Jerry and my secretary are constantly fussing over me, I must look awful."

Emotion produced a second quivering sigh. "I've missed you so much," she admitted, not looking at him. "I wanted to tell you about the baby right away.... I'd learned I was pregnant the afternoon you moved out. I came home from the doctor's office to find you packing."

"And you didn't tell me then?" he bellowed.

It was a mistake to have admitted she'd known about the baby before he left, especially then. "Would it have changed anything if I had told?"

"Yes," he answered automatically, then scowled and lowered his gaze. "I don't know."

"I'd hurt you and was hurting so badly myself. If I'd told you about Junior, then I feared it might have sounded like blackmail."

"You realize now that I would never betray you?"

"I knew it then, I always knew it ... I just did a poor job of showing you how much I love and trust you." A teardrop ran from the corner of her eye and dangled from the end of her nose. "No words can ever express how sorry I am for the pain I caused you. When we married, I didn't expect to fall in love with you. I'd steeled myself against it. I'd been in love once before and the experience had cost me and others dearly.

"A green-card marriage seemed workable. I was determined not to involve my heart, but day after day you were there calling me your love, chipping away at my defenses no matter how hard I fortified them.

"When Ruth died ... I don't think I would have survived that time without you. Your comfort and love meant the world to me. I'll always treasure our day at the beach.

"After everything that's happened, I don't know if that makes any sense.... It probably doesn't." She stopped to gather her breath and to keep her voice from cracking. "This much is a fact—I love you, Alek, and I'm deeply sorry for the hurt I caused you. I swear, I'll never doubt you again." Tears fell unheeded from her eyes, marking her cheeks.

"Don't cry, Julia."

She noticed he didn't call her *my love* the way he had so often in the past. Covering her face with her hands, she wiped away the moisture, expelled a wobbly sigh and forced herself to smile. "I know it's a lot to ask, but could you ever find it in your heart to forgive me for contacting Roger that day?"

"If you can forgive me for letting my pride stand in the way?"

"Your pride? Oh, Alek, I trampled over it a hundred times, and still you loved me. I didn't know how to deal with love and I made so many mistakes."

"I made my own mistakes."

"I asked Anna about you countless times, but she refused to talk about you. I don't think she's forgiven me for hurting you."

"Ah, my sister," Alek said slowly. "She played the same game with me. I asked her about you so often that she finally told me if I was so curious, I should go ask you myself."

"She was right, you know. Neither one of us had any business putting her in the middle, pumping her for information about the other."

"I agree. But I still don't like it that you didn't tell me about our baby."

Julia thought her heart would melt at the tender way he said *baby*. Alek was going to be a wonderful father. She hadn't gone into the marriage with any great expectations other than she didn't anticipate being married long. Falling in love with Alek had come as a welcome, wonderful surprise.

His tenderness, his patience, his comfort had seen her through those bleak days surrounding Ruth's final days and the dark weeks that followed. Without him, she feared she would have become a lost, tormented soul. How wise Ruth was to recognize the type of man Alek was, and what an excellent choice he was for her husband.

"I would have eventually found a way of getting in touch with you," Julia admitted, "Soon, too.... I don't know how much longer I would have been able to keep the baby to myself." She stopped talking, realizing Alek had come to her because he'd learned of her condition. Slowly she raised her eyes to his. "Who told you I was pregnant?"

If Jerry had known where Alek was all this time, she swore she'd have her brother's hide.

"Does it matter who told me?"

"Yes."

"All right, if you must know, a private detective told me."

"You hired a private detective to...?"

"No, apparently Jerry was the one who did the hiring. Your brother thought it was my right to know about the baby."

It didn't escape Julia's notice that he still hadn't referred to her as his love.

"I see," she said slowly. "And now that you know about the baby, what do you expect to happen?"

He frowned, as though he disliked the question. "That depends on several matters."

"Yes?" she pressed when he didn't immediately respond. "What sort of matters?"

"I'll expect to be a major part of our child's life."

Julia nodded in full agreement; she was hoping he'd be a major part of her life, too. "I'd like that. Is there anything else?" she asked when he didn't continue.

Alek seemed to need time to think over his response. "I'd very much like to be your husband, to live with you and love you and have another child, perhaps two, depending on how you feel. Would this be agreeable to you?"

She nodded wildly, throwing her arms around his neck with such eagerness that she nearly toppled the chair he was sitting on.

"Be careful, my love...."

"Say that again." She choked out the words through her tears. "Call me your love. Oh, Alek, I've missed hearing that so much. Wait, kiss me first. I adore it when you say it when you're feeling loving." Apparently she had so many requests he didn't know which one to comply with first. It didn't take him long, though, to direct her mouth to his.

"My love."

"Oh, Alek."

"Julia."

Their names were trapped between two hungry mouths. Between two eagerly beating hearts.

Their mouths strained toward each other. Julia felt the emotion bubble up within her. She'd missed him so much, much more than she dared admit even to herself, much more than it was possible to realize. He was speaking to her in Russian, short snatches of words between hungry kisses.

She tightened her arms around his neck and moved her torso against his chest.

He surprised her by standing and carrying her into the bedroom. "You are so wonderfully romantic," she told him, languishing in his arms as he carried her toward their bedroom.

"I plan to get a whole lot more romantic in about thirty seconds." His intentions were clear as he lovingly laid her across the top of her mattress.

"Oh good.... Hurry, Alek, I've needed you so much."

He stripped while she watched him, marveling at his maleness and his hard readiness for her. Sitting up, Julia struggled out of her T-shirt and tossed it aside. Her tennis shoes came next. "I really should shower," she commented as the spandex pants flew in the opposite direction.

"There's no time for that now," Alek said impatiently. "Later, we'll shower together."

"But I just finished a workout."

"And you're about to start another," he said as he gripped her hands and pressed her back into the folds of the mattress, his mouth and tongue teasing hers. His mouth, his wonderful, sexy mouth was a seduction all of its own. He drugged her with need, promised her the heavens and then fulfilled his word by taking her to the stars and back.

They were exhausted, panting in each other's arms several minutes later, their bodies linked, their hands and hearts entwined.

"You feel so damn good," Alek whispered, his eyes hazy with passion. "I must have forgotten how good, otherwise I would have been back that first night." He eased his mouth to hers. The kiss was sweet and gentle.

A tear slipped from the corner of her eye. "You've got to quit saying beautiful things like that, or I'll start crying all over again."

"Perhaps I should show you how I feel instead." He lowered his face to her breasts and nuzzled their swollen softness with his nose before claiming the hardened peak with his lips. She arched against him as his mouth took in the whole of her nipple and sucked greedily.

She felt his arousal harden and fill her completely. This man never ceased to amaze her. She brought her hips up and against his, loving the sound of his moan.

"I love you, Alek."

"You are my love," he returned as their bodies greedily met and satisfied each other.

Julia slept in her husband's arms afterward, her head upon his chest. When she stirred awake, she found his hand pressed against her abdomen and heard him communicating in whispers to his child. Since he was speaking in Russian, she was left to speculate what he was saying.

He found her looking at him and smiled shyly. "I told him to be good to his mother."

"Him?"

"A daughter would satisfy me, as well. Someday a young man will come to me and thank me for having fathered such a beautiful daughter. Wait, and you'll see that I'm right."

"Someday a young woman will come to me and tell me our son is totally awesome, or whatever vernacular is popular at that time. It changes every few years, you realize."

"I sometimes want to go crazy with things you Americans say. I fear I will be forever lost in your language because it's constantly changing."

"You're not lost, Alek. You've been found. By me. Don't worry, you'll catch on. I'll help you, we'll help each other."

"I've found myself in you, Julia. Never again will I leave you."

They showered and Julia dressed in a thick terry-cloth robe and padded barefoot into the kitchen. "I don't know about you, but I'm starved."

Alek grinned. "I see your appetite has increased."

Julia hadn't realized it, but it was true. "I suppose it has." She opened the refrigerator and took out a container of ice cream and served them both up large bowls.

"Should we call Jerry?" Alek asked. "We seem to owe him a good deal."

"No, I don't want to share you with anyone just yet. Tomorrow will be soon enough."

They sat in the living room, cuddled against each other, eating their ice cream. "The late news is on," Julia commented. "Do you mind if I turn it on?"

"No, not at all." He took the empty ice-cream bowl from her hand and set it aside. Then he brought her back against him and cupped her swollen breasts in the palms of his hands. "As long as you don't mind my minor distractions.'' He flexed his thumb over her nipple and she bit into her lower lip at the whirl of sensation that shot through her.

"I try to keep up with current events as much as I can," she said as a means of keeping her mind on the subject at hand. "I missed the earlier newscast because I had a doctor's appointment."

Alek's gaze widened with concern.

"It was the dentist, don't worry." She leaned forward and reached for the remote control. The screen blossomed to life just as the sportscaster finished with the latest update. It was heaven to sit with Alek's arms around her, more heaven than she dreamed.

"I will take our son to baseball games," Alek announced, "and the library."

"I hope you intend on taking your daughter and your wife while you're at it."

"Whoever wishes to go," he said, as though their family were already complete and they were deciding on a means of entertainment to satisfy everyone.

Julia smiled softly to herself.

After the sports news, they were given the five-day weather forecast. "I hope it rains every day," Alek whispered close to her ear. "That way I can keep you inside, or better yet, in our bed."

"I've got news for you," Julia whispered, kissing his cold, ice-cream-covered lips. "You don't need an excuse to take me to bed. In case you haven't noticed, I'm crazy about you."

"I noticed," he said with a satisfied smile. "And I approve."

Soon they were kissing again. They would have continued thus, Julia was certain, if the newscaster hadn't returned to announce the breaking news stories of the day.

"Ideal Paints, a national paint manufacturer, based here in Seattle, has declared bankruptcy. As many as three hundred jobs lost."

Julia was stunned. "I knew they were having financial difficulties," she said, breaking away from Alek. "I just didn't realize it was that serious."

"They couldn't hope to compete with Conrad Industries any longer," Alek explained. "Stanhope hurt them, but it took them this long to feel the effects. Their whole developmental program came to a halt after he sold them the formula for guaranteed twenty-five-year paint. They had the latest advancement without having gone through the learning process, without the trial and error that comes with any major progress. It set them back five years."

Julia had never thought of it in those terms. What she did remember was something Ruth had told her years earlier when revenge and justice had ranked high on her motivation list. Her grandmother had insisted time had a way of correcting injustices. Her wonderful Ruth had insisted time wounds all heels, and she'd been right.

"I wonder what will happen to Roger," she said absently, almost feeling sorry for him.

"He's finished in the business world," Alek stated calmly. "It's a well-known fact he sold out Conrad Industries. The word is out and no company is going to risk hiring an employee with questionable loyalty and ethics. He'll be lucky to find any kind of employment."

"Everything's come full circle," Julia said, leaning against her husband's strength. He wrapped his arms around her waist and she pressed her hands over his. "All that I lost has been returned to me a hundred fold."

Alek kissed her neck. "And me."

"I didn't know it was possible to be this happy. Only a few years ago I felt as if my whole life were over and now it seems to get better and better each day." Arching her back, she looped her arms around her husband's neck and reached upward for his kiss.

*   *   *   *   *

Look for Bride Wanted *by Debbie Macomber, the next book in* FROM THIS DAY FORWARD. *Coming in September from Special Edition.*

Silhouette

SPECIAL EDITION®

From this day forward

Coming in August,
the first book in an exciting new trilogy from
Debbie Macomber
GROOM WANTED

To save the family business, Julia Conrad becomes a "green card" bride to brilliant chemist Aleksandr Berinski. But what more would it take to keep her prized employee—and new husband—happy?

FROM THIS DAY FORWARD—Three couples marry first and find love later in this heartwarming trilogy.

Look for
Bride Wanted (SE #836) in September
Marriage Wanted (SE #842) in October

Only from Silhouette Special Edition

Fifty red-blooded, white-hot, true-blue hunks from every State in the Union!

Beginning in May, look for MEN MADE IN AMERICA! Written by some of our most popular authors, these stories feature fifty of the strongest, sexiest men, each from a different state in the union!

Two titles available every other month at your favorite retail outlet.

In September, look for:

DECEPTIONS by Annette Broadrick (California)
STORMWALKER by Dallas Schulze (Colorado)

In November, look for:

STRAIGHT FROM THE HEART by Barbara Delinsky (Connecticut)
AUTHOR'S CHOICE by Elizabeth August (Delaware)

You won't be able to resist MEN MADE IN AMERICA!

by Lindsay McKenna

Morgan Trayhern has returned and he's set up a company full of best pals in adventure. Three men who've been to hell and back are about to fight the toughest battle of all...love!

You loved Wolf Harding in HEART OF THE WOLF (SE #817) and Sean Killian in THE ROGUE (SE #824). Don't miss Jake Randolph in COMMANDO (SE #830), the final story in this exciting trilogy, available in August.

These are men you'll love and stories you'll treasure...only from Silhouette Special Edition!

by Laurie Paige

Come meet the wild McPherson men and see how these three sexy bachelors are tamed!

In HOME FOR A WILD HEART (SE #828) you got to know Kerrigan McPherson. Now meet the rest of the family:

A PLACE FOR EAGLES, September 1993—
Keegan McPherson gets the surprise of his life.

THE WAY OF A MAN, November 1993—
Paul McPherson finally meets his match.

Don't miss any of these exciting titles—only for our readers and only from Silhouette Special Edition!

It takes a very
special man to win
That Special Woman!

She's friend, wife, mother—she's you! And beside each Special Woman stands a wonderfully special man. It's a celebration of our heroines—and the men who become part of their lives.

Look for these exciting titles from Silhouette Special Edition:

August MORE THAN HE BARGAINED FOR by Carole Halston
Heroine: Avery Payton—a woman struggling for independence falls for the man next door.

September A HUSBAND TO REMEMBER by Lisa Jackson
Heroine: Nikki Carrothers—a woman without memories meets the man she should never have forgotten...her husband.

October ON HER OWN by Pat Warren
Heroine: Sara Shepard—a woman returns to her hometown and confronts the hero of her childhood dreams.

November GRAND PRIZE WINNER! by Tracy Sinclair
Heroine: Kelley McCormick—a woman takes the trip of a lifetime and wins the greatest prize of all...love!

**December POINT OF DEPARTURE by Lindsay McKenna
(Women of Glory)**
Heroine: Lt. Callie Donovan—a woman takes on the system and must accept the help of a kind and sexy stranger.

Don't miss THAT SPECIAL WOMAN! each month—from some of your special authors! Only from Silhouette Special Edition!

TSW3